JUSTICE SEEKERS

ORIGIN
OF THE
BLACK
DRAGON

CARLOS TORRES

Justice Seekers: Origin of The Black Dragon

©2023, Carlos Torres

ISBN: 978-1-66788-840-8

ISBN eBook: 978-1-66788-841-5

ACKNOWLEDGMENT

I WOULD LIKE to thank Daryel and Ronda McCurry, and Jace and Lesli Honey for having me at their La Junta, CO Livestock Commission Open House Anniversary, for a book signing. They have been instrumental in their support with the ranching community, and helped get the word out about my first book, *"Justice Seekers."* They inspired me to include them in my sequel, *"Justice Seekers the Origins of The Black Dragon."* The book is fiction, as are all the incidents and characters within, with the exception of Daryel and Jace.

CONTENTS

1

MAKING THE BLACK DRAGON

AKIO KATSUMI HAD just killed three men of the Yakuza, a known criminal organization of Japan. It was the end of the Festival of the Dragon; his wife Akemi was killed five years prior, by a Yakuza gang member. He had asked for help from the local gang and was laughed at and run out of town. Akio had traveled the country asking martial arts school masters to teach him martial arts fighting. After learning from one school, he would move on to another school; he did this several times. He paid his way by cleaning, cooking, and doing the laundry for the schools. Akio had much to learn as he had been hurt several times while fighting the men of the Yakuza. He decided to go to China to learn more fighting styles before he continued his quest for vengeance. Akio asked the Captain of a fishing vessel to work on his boat to pay for his passage to China. The Captain of the boat agreed because he was down a few men to man the nets. The trip to Shanghai was longer than he wanted; two weeks at sea made him yearn for dry land and he had been losing weight from the lack of food and being sea sick most of the time.

The city of Shanghai was much bigger than he had imagined. He found himself looking for shelter but was turned away because he was from Japan with no money or a job. He found himself begging on the street for food and walked for miles looking for shelter. He found solace on the river banks where he tried fishing for his food. It was on the river banks that he met a Shaolin monk and shared his fresh catch of a few fish. Akio told the monk his story of heartbreak, revenge, and his training. The monk spoke to Akio about purpose in life and asked him to what end did he look to fulfill his life. The monk left Akio sitting on the river bank looking at the flow of the river, allowing him to think of their conversation. The next several days, Akio would walk the streets and go back to the river bank to sleep and fish for his food. It was mid-morning when the monk showed up at the river bank and saw Akio fishing. The monk watched Akio catch and release several fish. Akio turned and asked if he was hungry. The monk smiled and said he would enjoy sharing a meal if he could explain the meaning in releasing the fish. Akio told the monk that he was learning the feeding times; he did not need more than he could eat, so he would release them. After having shared a meal with Akio, he asked if he would like to walk to the temple to meet with others and learn from them. Akio was very grateful and asked if he could cook or clean to earn his way to learn from them. The monk explained that the way to self-fulfillment through servitude, is sometimes a very long journey; revenge will only give temporary happiness, while justice will give you purpose.

It had been several months since his arrival at the monastery. The work was harder than he expected; carrying large water jugs from the river to fill the tubs of water for the animals and plants. The cooking and raking the grounds were a daily chore. Akio would watch the masters train their students and fellow monks for hours on end and he would train by himself in the dark of night. The months went by and soon he thought of his wife. It was time to find the Yakuza and take his revenge for a life stolen from him. Akio went out of the monastery after the day's work and walked for miles thinking about what he had learned; he was contemplating trying some of the new fighting techniques, but he was not sure of the finishing moves. Akio walked back to the monastery thinking about the monk's teaching. He had been hiding from the Yakuza in a monastery in China; he was not sure if he would live long enough to learn from Shaolin monks. He did not like hiding. He wanted to let the Yakuza know that he was responsible for the deaths of their members.

In the morning, he was met by the Shaolin monk that was responsible for his good fortune; he had a place to learn martial arts, eat, sleep and work. The monk told him that he had been seen outside the walls of the monastery last night. The monk asked him if he had a desire to leave before his training was over. Akio looked puzzled; he did not know that he was in training. No one had taken him aside to show him any moves that he had been copying late at night. The monk smiled and said, "Why would you take a fish out of the water, if it only knew how to swim?" The rest of the day went as always, bringing the water up from the river and raking the training yard; but instead of going to the kitchen to work, he was told to join the rest of the students in the training yard. When asked which style he would like to learn, he smiled and said, "All of them". The monk nodded his head and said, "Your formal training starts today."

Akio trained with the others and excelled fast within the ranks, being humble and always asking for guidance. He never complained. Akio studied the scrolls of the masters and continued to practice during the night; putting on specific lengths of rope tied to his ankles to get his foot position correct for each movement. The monks watched him and saw his dedication, as some students joined him at night perfecting their skills. This went on for months, which turned into years, as some students left and new students came. Akio was now assisting with the younger students in their training and now practiced with several weapons on a daily schedule. His thoughts were of discipline and knowledge; revenge was hidden away in the back of his mind now, only seeking justice as his future. He had purpose in training others and it felt good to him; he would soon go back to Japan and find his granddaughter to train her and teach her the ways of the Shaolin.

The night air was cool as Akio trained in the open yard. Four monks walked into the training area and surrounded him. Akio looked at the monks. Not knowing what to expect, he stood with his feet together and his head lowered, putting one hand over the other. A monk told him that his training was nearly over and now he had to learn the way of the Dragon. Akio explained that he knew nothing of this style, as there were no writings about it and saw no training. The monks explained that they were the Dragon. He was to learn from the four of them and put all their teachings into one form. No one person had ever been able to master the moves in one hundred years, but the monks thought that he may be the one to master the moves, known as the Dragon. Akio was honored and accepted the challenge to learn the four styles to become the Dragon; but it required him to stay longer at the monastery.

Night after night, Akio and the monks trained in the cover of darkness, away from the other students. Akio was understanding the moves and the force used to achieve the right hitting distance; he was becoming a weapon with his hands and feet, but was having trouble with the spinning speed to master the Dragon's Tail. One of the monks brought out some bands and put them on his hands and feet, and told him to close his eyes and let his mind follow the moves. The monk put his hands and feet together with Akio's, as he started the moves. They moved as one, slowly and then sped up the moves until Akio had the moves by memory; another monk took the others place and went through the same training, only adding his own new moves. All four monks had been together with Akio sharing their knowledge of the

Dragon. It was now up to Akio to put together the moves of the Dragon in the correct order, to get the results needed to do the Dragon's Tail.

After weeks of practicing at night, Akio thought he was ready and asked the monks to test him. They met in the center of the courtyard where the sand was soft and footsteps would be hidden from sound. Akio stood in the center of the circle and put on a blind fold; the monks watched as he readied himself. Akio's moves were like an animal; twisting and turning, moving in and out; the monks went on the attack, one at a time, then two, and finally, all four. Several times one or two of the monks would be hit by Akio's fist or feet. When all four came, Akio turned and jumped into the air twisting so fast, he was a blur and hit all four of the monks before they could touch him. Akio landed on his feet softly, and moved slowly as if he were hunting for a target. The monks were surprised at his speed and his movements; they saw the Dragon's Tail and all the moves. Akio had mastered the Dragon.

The monks gathered around Akio and told him that his training was over and he was ready to leave the monastery. Akio was grateful and showed respect towards his teachers and friends. The head of the monastery told him if he or any of his descendants came to the monastery, they would be welcome; but to bring an open mind to learn. He gave Akio a black sash with some symbols that told the story of the Dragon. Akio was honored and packed a few things together for his journey home. Two monks walked on both sides of Akio, thinking that they were going to escort him out of the monastery; but instead, they took hold of his arms and pulled down his robe over his arms. Akio was not sure what was going on but he did not struggle and walked with them to a small area in the monastery. The room was dark and hot; then he saw the red-hot kettle with burning coals under it. The head monk explained that he must carry the symbol of the Black Dragon on his chest for the rest of his life and breath in the fire as the Dragon. Akio was frightened and did not understand what that meant. The two monks released his arms; Akio had to be willing to bare the symbol of the Dragon of his own free will. Akio saw the raised relief of the dragon on the kettle; it was red-hot and sweat started to roll down his face onto his chest. Before his courage failed him, he stepped into the symbol of the Dragon and screamed in pain, feeling as if the fire was coming out of his chest. As Akio stepped away from the kettle, two monks held up his arms and chest, preventing him from collapsing, while the head monk put a salve on his chest. It was very cool, almost cold. He did not feel the pain any longer; the smell of eucalyptus and tea came to mind. The monk gave him a small white jar of the salve and told him to put it on his chest twice a day and on the third day he would no longer need it. It was going to aid in the healing process for all his wounds in the future. Akio walked out of the monastery with the feeling of purpose and held his head high as he walked to the fishing docks.

Akio stood at the dock looking for a fishing vessel that he could work on to earn his way back to Japan. He was in luck when an old man asked if he wanted to work on a small fishing boat. Akio did not hesitate and said, "Yes," before he saw the boat. It was truly a small fishing boat fit for only two or maybe three men. The old man smiled and told him they would leave in the next tide out. Late that afternoon, the old man saw him and asked, "Why didn't you walk away when you saw the boat?" Akio looked at him and said, "It was not about the boat, but the journey." The old man smiled and told him to get on board and untie the ropes from the dock. The old man turned down the sails from the mast and took control of the rudder; the boat caught some wind and went out to sea. The fresh, salty air felt good against Akio's face as he looked at the sea in front of him. After a while, the old man told Akio to be ready to put the nets into the water; the fish should be in the area off the point of the bay. Akio suddenly realized that they were not going to Japan, they were was just fishing. In his haste, he failed to ask for passage to Japan; he just accepted to work for the old man. Akio thought he had acted too hastily with the old man but felt he had to see it through and help him. It was not long before the nets were full and the boat was leaning to one side. The old man said he had never seen the nets so full before and he was in good fortune. It took both Akio and the old man to pull the nets into the boat; the boat was full. The old man was very happy and told Akio that he would have a good payday.

The old man docked the boat and several men walked up the see the catch; it was indeed the best catch of the day by any one boat. They all helped the old man unload the fish with baskets in hand and put the fish in a large cart to take to market. Akio felt that he had done a good thing by helping the old man, but had learned to choose his words more carefully. As Akio stepped onto the dock, his robe opened just enough so that his fresh red burn scar was showing; one of the dock workers saw it and turned away. The old man had also seen the burn and looked away. Akio adjusted his robe to cover the burn as some of the dock workers walked away from Akio. The old man took Akio to the side and told him that he had seen the burn on his chest as did another man. Akio did not know what all the fuss was about and why it caused so much attention. The old man said it was about a legend of a man who would bring justice wherever he went, and that the criminals would fear him; only the Shaolin knew of the powers that he possessed. Akio reassured the old man the he had no special powers, but the old man told him to look at the fish they caught saying, "Tell me you have no powers." Akio could not convince the old man otherwise. That evening, Akio sat at the dock waiting for the old man to show up so he could ask if he knew of any boat that could take him to Japan.

The moon was full, as Akio sat on the edge of the dock looking at the sea. He heard several steps of men walking behind him. As Akio turned to see faces of the men, he was aware that the moon was at his back and he was but a dark silhouette on the edge of the dock. Akio saw the flash of knife blades in their hands. He said, "I seek you no harm; all I need is passage to Japan." A large man said, "All I seek is your blood." Akio told them to, "Come if you must, but I will dance in your blood and stand on your bones before I die, for I am the Black

Dragon." Akio heard blades drop on the dock and running feet, but a few still stayed to test him. A large man started waving his knife in back-and-forth motion across his body; it was a common move for the untrained. Akio moved without effort; the knife missing on every stroke. The man was already growing tired after several tries and was clearly winded. Akio grabbed the man's arm and threw him into the sea. There was no need to kill him; he had to learn to swim before he could fight. The other men saw that it was no effort for the stranger to throw their leader into the sea. They had to save face for their leader and they rushed the man called the Black Dragon. Akio side-stepped them and threw them into the water; one by one, telling them they had to learn to swim. No blood was spilled and compassion was shown. As Akio walked away from the dock, he thought about the words that he had used; it came from within, without any effort and it felt natural. There was no anger. The right amount of justice was served this time; it was their fear of the unknown that was their undoing. Akio walked off the dock and into the night. He would try to find a boat in the morning.

In the early hours of the morning, Akio found the old man near his boat. He had been tortured; his fingers were cut off, bleeding from multiple stab wounds and was near death. The old man said that the big man from last night was a Triad leader that controlled the docks and he wanted to know everything about the man who had thrown him off the dock. The old man said, "I told him nothing, but he and his men cut my fingers off and stabbed me, leaving me here to die." Akio told the old man not to worry as he would bring justice to the men that harmed him. The old man smiled and said, "Tell me again that you have no powers." The old man died in Akio's arms. Several people from the area saw the old man and asked Akio if they could take him to his family to be laid to rest. Akio nodded and let a few men carry the body away, and asked for someone to show him the way to the leader of the docks; all they did was point in the direction of the last dock of the bay.

The shack at the end of the pier had a large boat tied to the dock with a small wooden plank serving as a walkway to the boat. This was not a fishing boat, but a boat used for smuggling or for pirates. Akio walked calmly towards the shack, not really knowing what to expect; but he knew of nothing that would stop him. A man came out of the shack yelling for Akio to stop. Akio kept walking and looked at the boat asking if it was sea worthy enough sail to Japan. Men came running down the wooden plank onto the dock; the last man was the large man that he had thrown into the sea the night before. The large man yelled at Akio saying that he was lucky last night, but today he would join the old man and die. Akio lowered his head and slowly walked towards the first man holding a pair of large knives. The man looked back to the others, waiting to see what to do when the large man ordered them to kill Akio. As the man turned to charge, Akio was already inches away from him. The man was surprised as Akio hit him across the throat with his blade hand; it crushed the man's throat. The man went to his knees with gurgling sounds coming from his throat choking on his own blood. Akio took the knives and held them out, away from his body with his head tilted down and showed no emotion. The men on the dock looked nervous as Akio walked towards them; he was now starting to spin in circles with the knife blades out becoming a blur. The men started to fall one at a time; sometimes two, with multiple cuts across their faces and throat. Blood was everywhere on the dock as Akio continued to spin in the blood, kicking it in the faces of the remaining men standing, who were watching, and now trembling with fear. They fell to the dock dead, with stab wounds to the chest. The large man was last, as he looked on at the carnage below him. All his men were dead. The large man yelled at Akio wanting to know his name. "What is your name? I want to know who I am killing." Akio looked up at the man on the boat and said, "I am the Black Dragon, seeking justice for the old and weak." The large man was nervous and looked down for a second to grab his black-powder pistol; when he looked up, Akio was gone; no longer standing on the dock. The startled man turned around to look for Akio and felt a knife enter his stomach and another knife at his hand holding the pistol. Akio cut the hand off at the wrist and watched as the big man was without words as he slid the knife across his liver. Akio kicked the man into the water and watched as the fish came up to pick at the pieces of flesh in the water. Justice had been served for the old man and his family.

The old man's family and some volunteers took the pirate ship and offered to take Akio to Japan. They would scuttle the ship outside of the bay upon their return to China.

It had been many years since Akio had walked on his home soil. He had a long walk to his village to find his son and granddaughter. It was as the monks had said; his Dragon scar had healed in three days; but the scar was black from the iron in the kettle. He thought it wise to keep the scar hidden from others. He wrapped himself in a soft bandage and wore a shirt and robe and kept it closed tight. The walk through the countryside was peaceful, but some of the fields had become over-grown and unattended. Akio saw that some of the small homes had been burned down and abandoned; he could not understand why someone would cause such damage. A small village that had been thriving with people and children was now run down with closed shops and walls half-built around the entrance near the road. A few old women walked the streets. The only shop open was busy; it was a small bar with a few tables that were filled by men wearing swords, drinking rice wine and gambling. Akio walked slowly past the men as they drank their wine. One of the men put his sword across the path of Akio and asked, "Where are you going and where did you come from?" Akio kept his head down and said, "I am but a stranger passing through, looking for my granddaughter." The man laughed saying, "You must pay to pass through this town; sorry, these are not my rules." "I do not have money; I am but a poor traveler trying to find my family," replied Akio. "How do you eat?" asked the man, tapping his sword on the wooden floor. "I gather greens from the fields, fish from the rivers and ask for work to earn my way." "So, what would you offer to make your way through this village? You have no money, so you must work until I say you have earned your way through," said the man, now standing in front of Akio. The other men at the tables were laughing and told him to start by bringing them more wine and to clean the floors and tables. Akio looked around and asked, "Who would I be taking orders from here?" The man with the sword looked at the others and said, "That would be me. I am in charge here." An old woman came out from behind a curtain with a straw broom and tried to hand it to Akio, but the man with the sword pushed her back and told her to find more wine and food or she will be talking with her ancestors at the end of the road.

Akio looked at the man and asked, "What would you have me do for passage?" The man stood there thinking and looking at Akio as to size him up. "You look strong and healthy, so I will use you for training practice; if you live, you can go on your way; if you die, you join the others at the end of the road." Akio looked at him and asked, "What if you die and I live?" The other men at the tables laughed, "Then you will have to kill us." They told their leader to make good sport of him and not to kill him too quickly. The leader showed Akio to the center of the road and threw him the broom that the old lady had dropped. Akio looked at the man and asked if he could inspect his weapon as he picked up the broom. All the men laughed and told him to be careful. Akio took off the straw from the end and now held a six-foot pole. Akio twirled the pole and it made a buzzing sound; he stopped and held the pole in his arm and looked at the man with the sword and gave a nod of his head. The man smiled and said, "So you are trained, good, it will make for better practice." Akio stood watching the man move with the sword; he was trained as a samurai or had some type of formal training. He came at Akio taking short chopping movements and then went into a defensive stance. Akio stood with the pole, holding it out with one arm, when the man started his attack again. Akio vaulted himself into the air holding on to the pole and swung the pole down with both hands. The pole hit the top center of the man's head and it split open like a ruptured melon. The men had watched in horror as Akio slid the pole out the skull. The man's body fell in a pile, as the sword hit the ground. Men ran out of the little shack screaming, with knifes and swords in their hands. Akio stood with the pole behind his back waiting for the first man to come into range of the pole. It was not long before a small man with a large block knife, used to cut through bone, came swinging it wildly at Akio. Akio side-stepped him and turned, spinning with the pole hitting the man in the mouth; the man lost several teeth and was bleeding badly. Akio spun again and hit the man behind the head with such force it broke the skull, and blood spilled on the ground. Men were all around him swinging their swords and knives missing their mark. Akio made a circle in the dirt with the pole and stood in the middle; as a man would enter the circle, he would use the end of the pole to hit them in the eyes or mouth. Teeth were now sticking to the end of the pole. An attack came from behind. Akio was fast as he used the pole to vault himself on the other side of the circle and out of harm's way. His attackers were slowing down; many of them injured; but they kept trying to kill Akio. The skills of Akio were no match for the few men that were still standing, so he laid down his pole. Akio told the men, "You have a choice; stop this mindless attack on me and you will live. If not, you will die here with your friends." The men looked at each other seeing that he was now without his pole and ran towards him screaming and swinging their weapons. Akio picked up a sword from the ground and jumped into the air spinning. The men had no chance to live; they had made their choice clear. Akio killed them; cutting off their arms and heads as they entered the spinning circle of death.

An old woman came walking out from the small shop and picked up the pole that was her broom and started to wrap straw around it. A few old men came out of hiding and looked at the dead men lying in the street. They went through the pockets of the dead and picked up all the weapons putting them in a cart. An old man asked Akio, "Who are you, stranger, that you would risk your life for us?" Akio looked at the old man and said, "I am the Black Dragon and I bring justice." The old man cried and said, "You are too late. They killed most of the village people and stole everything of value that we had; where were you two days ago? My wife and daughter were killed by these men. They are part of the Yakuza, and they control this region." Akio felt as if he had let the poor villagers down. The men he had just killed were but a small group of hundreds, maybe thousands, of Yakuza in the region. He had set his mind to reducing those numbers and bring justice to the region, but first, he must find his son and granddaughter. As he left, he saw the bodies at the end of the village. They had not even had a proper burial; they were just in a pile as if they were trash.

Akio walked away depressed, thinking about how he could have helped the villagers and thought about his wife, which brought back feelings of revenge. He had lost track of time and he needed to find the rest of his family before they were also killed. The Shogun had to be responsible for allowing the Yakuza to rape, rob and steal from the villages. The people looked to leaders to protect them for which they paid high taxes for that protection. Someone had to fight back, and that was Akio.

It was getting dark and there were no villagers in sight. He would have to walk into the forest and find a safe place to sleep. It was not a good idea to be seen from the road, as there were bandits always roaming the area looking for something to steal or eat. Akio walked into the forest looking for a suitable place to sleep, but away from the road; he was tired and wanted to reflect on his choices. Akio fell asleep dreaming of his wife Akemi and a different time so many years ago. His son, Haruto and granddaughter, Aoi, were the only family he had after his wife's death. His son Haruto had been staying with his uncle, helping plant fields of rice; it had saved his life that day. When Akio left to avenge his wife's death, he had asked his brother to watch over his son. It had been years when he heard that Haruto had taken a wife. He did not know the details of her family; only that she had a baby girl named Aoi.

The morning came with the sound of a fire crackling near his feet and the smell of hot tea. Akio sat up and felt dizzy as he looked around not knowing how he had slept so hard as to not hear or sense that others were around him. There were several men around him wearing all black with short swords and knives in their waistbands. They were the feared Shinobis of Japan. The word "ninja" is a Chinese term. They were of the Iga clan; a ninja that was trained in disguise, escape, concealment, explosives, medicine, and poisons, as well as more conventional forms of warfare, such as unarmed combat and using various forms of weaponry. They were trained to use many tools, such as scaling hooks and hand claws for climbing the most impossible walls, and the use of picks to open doors, secured chests, and money boxes. Iga ninja groups were a major mercenary force. Smaller groups existed in other parts of Japan, but in the Sengoku Era, ninja groups rose throughout Japan. There were two super groups; the Iga of Mie and the Koga of Shinga prefecture. A prefecture are governmental bodies of Japan which are larger than cities, towns, and villages. The former provinces of Japan were converted into prefectures between 1876 and 1879.

2

FINDING FAMILY

A MAN SAT across from Akio with only his eyes showing. He held a long dart in his hand and rolled it between his fingers. Akio knew that he had been darted sometime in the night, thus making him feel dizzy when he sat up. The man offered him some tea saying that the dart poison would dissipate faster if he sat still and drank some tea. The dart was only meant to make him sleep; not to kill him and he would be wise to move slowly. Akio accepted the tea and noticed that he had been searched; his robe had been opened with his scar partially exposed. "We had to search you for weapons. So what happened to you? Why did someone brand you?" Akio told him that it was personal and did not want to talk about his scar. The man stood up and asked Akio, "Why were you in the forest sleeping and why were you traveling alone in such a dangerous place?" Akio told him again, trying to stall for time, that he did not want to talk about his journey. Now several men stood next to Akio and told him that he was not free to leave until they had some answers. Akio could see that they were not amused at

Akio's lack of information. Akio asked for another cup of tea and told them to sit and listen to his story before passing judgment; he knew that they were not to be trifled with, as they were all deadly at their skills. Akio raised his cup of tea and said thank you as a sign of respect, and told them his name was Akio Katsumi. He explained that he was looking for his son and granddaughter after returning from China. He told them of his revenge on the Yakuza for the death of his wife. His quest for knowledge in the martial arts throughout Japan was not enough, which led him to China. Akio explained how he had trained with the Shaolin monks for years and his scar was a symbol of his training. He had earned the title, Black Dragon, and instead of revenge, he now sought out justice for the poor and helpless; it gave him purpose.

The small group of men in black gathered to talk among themselves. The leader of the men stood in front of Akio and took off his mask and smiled saying, "Welcome home, father. Your granddaughter, Aoi is doing well and in training. We have much to talk about. We had almost given you up for dead, but first we must move from here, can you stand?" Akio stood up and asked, "Haruto, how can this be? I have many questions for you". "Not now, father, we must go now," said Haruto. The group ran silently through the woods staying out of sight from the road and following a river. Akio was feeling much better moving with the group; he felt happy being with his son, even if he was a Shinobi. The group stopped to rest near the river's edge. Two men ran in opposite directions along the river's bank looking for any tracks that were not theirs. Haruto looked at his father and said, "You are well conditioned. You are not even breathing hard." "I have much to teach you about the Shaolin training," replied Akio. Haruto smiled and said, "My wife, Moriko, is the great granddaughter of Momochi Sandayu, who was the leader of the Iga clan, going back hundreds of years. I was trained by some of the best, to include my wife." Akio nodded and said he was impressed by his skills, but there was more to learn.

The two men came back to the group after scouting the banks of the river saying it was all clear and they would be back in camp by sunset. The group of Shinobis moving and running along the river's edge was nothing less than impressive; they were quiet, light-footed and well-disciplined. It was still light when the group walked into camp. They made good time and Akio did not slow them down. Moriko was in a small field with Aoi, with a long wooden staff teaching her the ways of her clan. Haruto and Akio stood next to each other watching, as Moriko would go through several moves correcting Aoi as she copied her. Haruto cleared his throat and held out his arms toward Moriko and little Aoi saying, "This is your grandfather, Aoi." Moriko walked until she was standing in front of Akio; her bow was slow and deliberate. Aoi looked at her grandfather and copied Moriko and did a slow bow and then hugged Akio's leg. Akio knelt and picked her up and held her saying that she looked like her grandmother. Moriko told Akio that she had heard of a man that took vengeance on the Yakuza and hunted them. She asked, "Is this true?" "Yes," replied Akio, "I am that man. I have traveled to China to learn new fighting styles and to return to find those that were responsible for Akemi's death. In doing so, I found purpose with the Shaolin and a powerful new fighting style, not practiced in a hundred years. I am the Black Dragon." Akio pulled his robe open, and showed the scar he accepted. "I seek justice for the weak, from criminals that would make them victims. I will bring fear at the thought of the Black Dragon looking for them." Haruto asked his father if he would be willing to show the clan some of his new styles after he had gotten some food and rest. Moriko told Akio it would honor them if he would train the clan in any new style that could be beneficial for its survival. Akio stated that he would like to talk to the clan leader; his teaching cannot be used for evil. Moriko and Haruto looked at him and said that they shared the leadership positions and they were but a small cell of the clan. Akio looked surprised and asked, "Where is your uncle? What has happened to our family?" Moriko explained the events that had occurred over the last ten years in Japan, with the rise of the criminal element in the cities. Haruto told his father that his uncle had been killed shortly after his disappearance from Japan. The Yakuza still search for you in the bigger cities. The Yakuza control the shipping yards and most of the gambling houses along the coast without any interference from the magistrate. We travel and stay in the shadows and gather information. We stay in small groups, so we do not draw attention to any one area.

Over the course of the next few weeks, the clan got to know the new stranger who was teaching them a new style of fighting. The clan decided to only call him the Black Dragon and not connect him to the clan leaders. Akio saw how well-disciplined and well-trained the clan was, with Mariko as their leader. It was easy to see why they followed her. Haruto was her right hand and took all the training seriously and was still learning what Mariko shared with him.

They were married, but she had the lineage that still had respect in the clan; she was a warrior first and foremost. Akio had asked to train Aoi in the evenings, away from the others. He saw the little girl's attention to detail. She was stubborn and never gave up, even when her training lasted for hours. Haruto said that she got that stubborn streak from her mother. Akio smiled and said it ran in the family.

One evening, Akio and Aoi sat by a small camp fire enjoying the night when Mariko ran up and grabbed Aoi, saying that the clan had been discovered and they had to move fast into the forest. Haruto was beside Mariko; many clan members were already blending into the dark of the forest. Akio sat by the fire not moving, with his long staff next to him. Akio told them to leave; he would stay back to find out who was after them. Mariko and Haruto left with Aoi in their arms.

It was not long, before a large group of men came into the camp yelling, with swords in hand, looking for anyone. Akio sat still and watched as he counted how many men came into the camp. Several men ran up to Akio ready to deal out death with their swords, held at the ready to take off his head. A small man dressed in a military uniform stepped up to Akio and asked, "Why didn't you run into the forest with the rest of the women?" Akio smiled and said, "I saw no women, only warriors surrounding you in the dark". The little man turned and looked into the forest. He was not amused at Akio's comments. He ordered that some men enter the forest to find anyone to be questioned. Akio looked at the small man and asked him, "What do you know about warfare?" The man was upset and gave a look at one of the men behind Akio. Akio moved to his left and the man behind him missed his mark; a death blow across his neck. The speed of Akio taking the sword away from the soldier and killing him was astonishingly fast, as he held the blade to the neck of the leader. The man did not flinch, but stood his ground looking at Akio asking, "Why are you sparing my life?" Akio smiled and asked him, "Who are you looking for and why did you pick a peaceful camp to disrupt its people; to torture or kill them?" "I have been ordered to find and bring in those responsible that have been attacking the villages in this region. A woman leads them.""How do you know a woman leads them?" asked Akio. "Who are you? I can see you are a man of skills?" asked the leader. "Tell your men to leave this area and never come back; they are not responsible for the deaths in the villages. The men you seek are already dead. They robbed and killed many of the villagers in this region. They were Yakuza; criminals that roam this region with impunity," said Akio. The military leader asked how he knew of the deaths of the Yakuza men. Akio told him that he had killed them all; he had brought justice to the village. Only a few villagers were left to live, so they could serve them wine and service them." The leader was not convinced of Akio's story. Akio looked at him and told him to gather his men and leave because he did not want to see bloodshed. The leader's men stood all around them with swords at the ready. "Command your men to leave the forest. You have all the information you need to report back to the magistrate," said Akio. The leader smiled and said, "Do not tell me what I should do," as he yelled for his soldiers to kill anyone in the forest. There was silence. Not a sound came from the forest, as the five men were silent; never to return from the forest. The leader was looking at the darkness when several figures in black walked to the edge of the forest; none of his soldiers came out.

Akio lowered his head and sword in front of the leader and said, "So be it. I will dance in your blood and stand on your bones before I die, for I am the Black Dragon." The leader's eyes widened with surprise as he drew his sword, but Akio had already cut him nearly in half from the shoulder to the center of his chest. Men from all sides stepped back to see their leader dead. Akio was moving in a small circle with the sword becoming a blur as men tried to kill him. There were nine men lying dead all around Akio, when he looked up to see Haruto and Mariko standing with the clan behind them. Little Aoi was hiding behind Mariko's leg. Mariko told Akio that the soldiers from the forest were dead; they had been darted. Haruto looked at his father and said, "I had no idea of the skills that you possess. You were faster than the eye could follow." "It is the way of the Dragon," replied Akio "I will teach the way to our family, so it may be passed on; but it may require a journey to China for each family member." "So be it," replied Haruto. One of the clan members had searched a few of the soldiers and found markings of the Yakuza on their necks; they were paid mercenaries.

The clan broke camp. They had stayed in one place for too long and it was time to meet with other clan members. Akio helped the group and carried Aoi to keep her close. She would be next in line for the Shaolin to teach; while she was still young, her training would take many years. They walked for several days and avoided villages and cities. They neared the mountains leading to the main village of the Iga clan. Word had gotten out that the Black Dragon was now in Japan. The Yakuza had many spies in the government and cities. They wanted the Black Dragon by any means necessary.

As the clan entered the village, many children ran up to Moriko and greeted her. Akio was holding Aoi's hand has she started to tug on his hand to let her be free to play with the other children. Haruto told Aoi to stay close and not to run off, as her grandfather let go of her hand. The Elder of the clan walked to Moriko and Haruto and greeted them. Akio stood next to his son and watched Aoi as the conversation started about the Black Dragon; he wanted to meet him. Akio stepped up to the Elder and bowed from the waist, showing respect saying, "I am the Black Dragon; the one you seek." Haruto stated to the Elder that Akio was his father that had gone missing for so many years. We are a family reunited once again. "Let us have tea and talk about the events that have led you to us," replied the Elder. As the group broke up into the village, the Elder walked them into a large training area. Akio was aware that he was going to be tested and stopped in the center of the yard.

"May I have the honor of meeting the Black Dragon?" asked the Elder. "I am not accustomed to showing my skills, but I have been known to share knowledge of my teachings," replied Akio. The Elder nodded and bowed at the waist saying, "Spoken like a Shaolin monk. I have heard stories of the Black Dragon out of China. Are they true? Do you have special powers?" "My power is knowledge and training; there is nothing special about hard work and dedication to one's belief," replied Akio. The Elder held up his hand. The arena was filling up with men dressed in black. Large drums were rolled out with women holding wooden sticks above the drums. This was turning out to be an event for the whole village, as the drums were now pounding out a slow rhythm. Three clan men dressed in black, joined Akio, Moriko and Haruto. They all faced each other and bowed from the waist. Akio smiled and thought that this was more than just a test of skill, but of trust; he would not hurt one member of the Iga clan.

A man walked out into the center of the arena with five wooden training swords and one wooden staff. The wooden staff was given to

Akio. The Elder clapped his hands together and the men in black ran to circle Akio. The drums stopped; all was quiet as the men moved into position, ready to press an attack on Akio. Akio lowered his head and nodded to his son and daughter-in-law; it was time to show his new fighting styles. The three men came in all at once. Akio planted his staff and vaulted over the men and tapped them on the back with his staff. The men were surprised at the speed in which Akio moved. Haruto and Moriko moved together trying to strike Akio from the front. They missed and were hit in the legs and arms with Akio's staff. The attackers were again pressing Akio and moved to strike him, but they missed and were hit once again by his staff. Akio now turned the tables on them; he pressed them by spinning his staff around his body and head; the air buzzed with the sound of his staff. Akio spun his staff in a circle and threw up sand and dust. Moriko and Haruto looked around and did not see Akio in the arena; only a staff stuck in the ground. As they walked towards the staff, the Elder clapped his hands together. Akio had been standing next to the Elder in a display of misdirection; a move that the Shinobis had been known to do. The three men, Moriko and Haruto stood looking at the Elder with Akio next to him. They could not explain how the Black Dragon had learned the moves of the Shinobis. That knowledge made him a worthy adversary by their standard, and very deadly. Akio had shown them a new style and the clan had been receptive to his demonstration of skills.

The Iga clan Elder and its members had many questions to ask of the Black Dragon. There were many days, and sometimes nights, that Akio would demonstrate certain moves and he would talk of the teachings of the Shaolin. The Elder told him of stories of the Black Dragon that had been passed on for generations from both China and Japan. The stories told of magic and wild tales of a dragon flying with fire and smoke to frighten its enemy. The stories were far from the truth, but they did have some truth to them.

Akio asked to stay with the clan to train them in better fighting styles, but also to learn from them to incorporate their styles into his own, which would make him better. The Elder of the clan wanted a stronger and more unpredictable Shinobis or ninja, and he agreed to send Haruto and Aoi to China to learn from the Shaolin, per the request of Akio. The teaching of the Shaolin was very important to Akio if he wanted the next generation of the Black Dragon to continue; especially if he was unable to find his wife's killers and bring justice to his family.

Moriko was not happy with the decision for Haruto and Aoi to leave the clan for China, but the Elder made the decision that was best for the clan and its future. In exchange, Akio would spend the rest of his time with the clan until their return. This was one of the many sacrifices that Moriko and Akio had to endure so they would be stronger, both mentally and physically. Akio would train Mariko in the ways of the dragon; after all, she was family.

Haruto and Aoi had been gone for almost a year. Moriko had been doing extremely well learning the moves of the Dragon. Now all she had to do, was join Akio and use the bands around their ankles and wrists. The test would also be to see if she could put all the moves together and use the Dragon's Tail. Akio needed more time to memorize the items needed in order to blend them to make the poisonous darts and the exploding bombs of smoke. Akio knew it was the time of the Dragon Festival. He would be looking for the Yakuza; looking for justice, not revenge. Akio would tell the clan Elder that he needed to leave for a few days in order to bring justice to his family. The clan Elder understood, and asked if he wanted some of the clan members to join him in his search for justice. Akio smiled and told him that this was his duty, as he bowed and left the Elder standing in the doorway.

Moriko over-heard Akio talking to the Elder and she had already made up her mind that she would follow Akio for his own safety. She was all dressed in black with some of her favorite weapons hidden on her waist and boots. She was running to keep out of sight of the Black Dragon, as he walked out of the village. Akio smiled to himself, knowing that Moriko was keeping pace with him. She was very silent and light on her feet; it was the way of the ninja. He was happy. She was family, and she knew that responsibility.

3

I AM NO MYTH OR FAIRY TALE

IT WAS LATE evening when Akio reached the edge of the city. He took a knee and spoke softly to Moriko to join him. Waiting several minutes, he felt a very slight breeze across his face and smiled; Moriko was next to him and took a knee. Moriko asked, "How long have you known that I was following you?" "Since I left the village," replied Akio. "I ask that you stay in the shadows. Do not attempt to stop me or help me; this is my duty to Akemi and I must follow my path." Moriko bowed her head and replied, "As you wish father," showing him respect. Moriko looked up and realized that he was gone.

Akio walked into the city with his wooden staff looking like a beggar. His head was lowered and wore a simple, black hood and tan robe wrapped around him with no weapons showing. Most of the small shops were closed; only the small bars and noodle stands were open. Akio noticed the noise and the smells of the city; he did not like them after being high in the mountains with fresh air and seeing stars in the night. It did not take long before he heard the loud laughing of men and the smell of wine. He stood by the door and listened to them talk; they were not the ones he was looking for tonight. As he slowly walked, he heard someone being slapped and a woman crying, and then the tearing of clothes. Akio followed the sounds to the back of a building; he saw a large, thick man smelling of wine and urine attempting to rape a young woman. She was fighting him off the best she could. The man grew tired of the woman and pulled out his sword to kill her, but instead, a wooden staff hit the top of his head crushing his skull. The woman watched as the man fell to the ground dead. She gathered up her robe and pulled it over her shoulders, which showed modesty, and thanked the stranger. Akio asked her, "Who was the man?" She said, "He was Yakuza and the rest of the men are inside the boarding house." She went on to tell him that the Yakuza had taken control at night and nobody was safe within the city. Akio told the woman to go home where she would be safe and not to return to the area; there would be many men looking for answers.

The boarding house was one building away from Akio; there were several men standing in the doorway laughing and looking for women to be victims of their evil ways. Akio slowly shuffled his way towards the men, stopped short of them and tapped the staff on the wooden walkway to get their attention. The men looked at him and laughed, making some lude comments until one of the men saw the blood on the end of his staff. A man drew his sword without any hesitation and asked him, "Where did the blood come from and who are you?" "If you are missing one of your friends, he is dead. I killed him because he was attempting to rape a young woman," replied Akio. The men looked at each other confused, and realized that one of their own was missing. They all drew their swords and waited for their leader to ask the stranger more questions. The leader asked Akio, "Who might you be, that you would boast of such an act that would cause your death?" "Do you not know that this is the last day of the Dragon Festival when the Black Dragon appears and kills members of the Yakuza?"

replied Akio. The men laughed and asked, "Is this some kind of joke?" "The joke would be on you; the Black Dragon seeks justice for your victims," replied Akio. The leader was not laughing. "Are you saying that you are the Black Dragon? That is just a myth or a fairy tale and I am not amused. Kill him!" The men went around the leader and after the old man standing with the wooden staff, but when they were about to deal a death blow, Akio planted the staff and vaulted over the men. Akio stood behind them and said, "I am the Black Dragon and I seek justice," as he took his robe off to show the black scar on his chest. The leader told him that his acrobatics and scar did not make him the Black Dragon. As he attacked Akio, his sword missed its mark. Akio reached behind his back and took out two short swords and held them out from his body saying, "I will have justice tonight." The men ran swinging their swords and missed Akio; he made them pay with their lives, cutting them several times before they fell dead. The speed of his attack surprised the leader and made him try even harder to kill him; but he missed and became frustrated by his effort by being cut every time he pressed his attack. Akio whispered to the leader, "I will dance in your blood and stand on your bones before I die." This just made the leader scream with anger, as he kept missing Akio. Akio started to spin with his short swords out. The leader was now fending off the attack as he heard the blades whipping through the air. The leader felt his arms and legs becoming heavy; he was bleeding out from all the cuts on his body. Akio stopped, did his kata, and kicked up blood on the leader's face. The leader watched as the Dragon did his kata. He did not feel the sword cut his throat, as his head rolled off his shoulders and hit the ground. Akio looked around and saw the carnage; twelve men lying in the street. He stepped on the leader's body as he walked out of the city and into the darkness.

Akio walked until he was near the river and walked into it to wash his clothes and body. Moriko sat near the river bank in silence. She knew the power of the Black Dragon, and saw for herself, the man she called father. When Akio was dressed, he sat next to Moriko. Moriko looked into her father's eyes and said, "I cannot begin to understand the pain you must feel for the loss of your wife at the hands of the Yakuza. I only know that I saw a man, known as the Black Dragon, exact justice upon those that deserved it; a man with dedication and skill. I am honored to be called daughter-in-law and I will continue your legacy." Off in the distance, they heard a bell ringing from the city; it was an alarm. They would have to travel fast to go back into the mountains.

Akio and Moriko walked into the village. It was still dark with only a few fires burning near the center of the village. This was not normal; something felt wrong and Akio stopped, looked around and did not seeing anyone. They both walked into the dark shadows of the night and watched the village. They saw a few dark shadows running from building to building and along the roof tops. Moriko told Akio that these intruders were hired ninja assassins. We must stop them and try to capture one of them, before he kills himself. Akio asked for her darts, which she carried in a small pouch, and a small bamboo tube. Akio told her to protect the Elder and not to spare anyone; he would take care of finding an assassin to interrogate. Akio took out his short swords and left in the direction of the ninjas. Moriko took to the roof tops to get to the Elder. She would try to blend in with the other assassins; the only thing different was the head wrap. Akio leaned against a wall and waited for a ninja to look around the corner of the building. As the assassin put his head around to see his location, Akio stuck him in the neck with a dart. The assassin fell to the ground. Akio pulled his body up and put him into a water barrel and closed the lid. Akio was on the target in seconds; a ninja, hiding in the trees overlooking the courtyard, was looking into the training area. Akio threw his sword up in an under hand motion and killed the ninja lying on a branch; the sword found its mark, going through the heart. Akio spun in a small circle and jumped up to grab his sword. The dead ninja stayed in the tree. Moriko ran along the roof tops and stopped in time to kill an assassin. She ran her sword into the back of his skull, before he jumped down at the Elder's doorway. His body fell at the entrance of the door. A clan member opened the door, just wide enough to drive a spear into the back of the dead man. Moriko whispered a chirping sound of a bird and the door opened; Moriko stepped inside to see all the clan members protecting the Elder. He was not unable to protect himself. He was armed with two swords and other weapons hanging from his waist. "The others are safe in the tunnels below the temple. We lost one young warrior that was on the perimeter, but not before he was able to shoot a flaming arrow to warn the village," said the Elder. Moriko told the Elder that Akio was hunting the assassins. One by one, the assassins fell; leaving a trail of blood to the next body. Akio looked back over his shoulder for just a fraction of a second, when he felt a small rope wrap around his right arm. The rope had small hooks that grabbed and tore into his arm, as the assassin pulled on the rope. Akio stepped into the rope to ease the tension and cut the rope with his free hand. His bleeding arm reminded him that he was still human, as he threw a smoke bomb down to create a diversion. The assassin came out to look for his adversary. He looked down to follow the blood when he should have been looking up to see Akio in the rafters looking down at him. Akio dropped down, and drove his sword to the hilt, into the assassin's head. Akio saw an assassin running from the walls towards the forest, when he saw that several white arrows had hit their mark in the middle of the assassins back; he fell, face-first into the dirt.

The attack was over and Akio retrieved the body from the water barrel, dragging him to the campfire. The Elder walked up to Akio and thanked him. He told him that he had saved many lives tonight. Moriko was standing next to Akio and saw his arm bleeding, and asked him how he was hurt? Akio told her of the rope-like weapon used with hooks. Moriko hurried home and told Akio to sit next to the fire until she came back. Akio felt somewhat dizzy and sat down. He knew that he had been poisoned. Akio sat with his legs crossed and started to meditate as he stared into the flames of the campfire. Moriko gave him some tea and put a lotion on his wounds. Akio showed no feelings and said nothing. The clan gathered around Akio and waited for something to happen; it was hours, but the tea was working, as sweat poured from Akio's face. His robe was wet with sweat, and his arm was red where the hooks had entered his arm. Akio blinked his eyes and told Moriko to go get the porcelain jar that was in his bed roll. Moriko did as he requested and brought the jar to him. Akio opened the jar and put the salve on his arm and told Moriko to wrap it. Moriko was concerned that she acted too late to save his life and gave him more tea with anti-venom. Akio sat with his legs crossed and stared into the fire until morning. Moriko sat with him and fell asleep next to her father-in-law, known as the Black Dragon.

Akio watched the sun rise and looked down into the eyes of the ninja; he was alive, but not moving. Then, he saw a dart sticking out of his neck. Moriko had darted him sometime in the night. Akio felt Moriko next to him; she had not moved all night. She had stayed to monitor him. The campfire was a pile of white coals now, and Akio heard members of the clan walking near him. He did not want to wake Moriko, but waited until the clan made their presence known. He heard small children running and giggling as they got closer. Moriko woke up and looked around to see the ninja; then she turned and saw Akio watching the ninja. Members of the clan gathered around Akio. The children poked a stick into the ninja, trying to make him move. The clan Elder arrived and thanked Akio again for helping save the people in the village, and asked how he was feeling? Akio stood up with Moriko, helping to keep him steady on his feet. He was still recovering from the poison, but his arm was no longer red and swollen. A woman from the clan gave Akio some fresh tea and a small rice ball to eat; another gave him some fish and vegetables that had been steamed. Akio bowed from the waist and thanked them.

4

THE NEXT DRAGON

THE CLAN ELDER looked down at the ninja, bent down on his knees and said, "Let's find out who sent you and what clan you are from." The ninja did not move, even when his head wrap was removed; he was searched and stripped. Moriko said that the ninja should be able to speak, but not move quickly. The Elder reached down and grabbed his jaw to force his mouth open. He saw that he had no tongue and then turned his head and looked behind his ear to see a marking. The Elder stood up, reached into his robe, and took out a knife saying, "This assassin was sent to kill us or die trying. I will help him on his journey," as he bent down and drove his knife into the base of the assassin's skull. "We will send a message to the outlaw clan that was hired to kill us." The Elder ordered that the bodies of the dead be put in a cart to be taken back to the outlaw clan. Akio looked at the Elder and said, "Justice will be served. I will be ready in two days." The Elder gave him a nod and walked away. He was very upset and he had reason; the outlaw clan's leader, Amura, was a relative of the magistrate.

Akio felt some urgency in his recovery. He knew that there could be a conflict between the clans, or worse. The magistrate could bring soldiers into the mix and try to wipe out the Iga clan completely. The question was who was behind this move? Moriko wanted to change Akio's bandage and see how his arm was healing. She asked him to sit while she got clean bandages and salve to put on his arm. Akio sat down feeling a little sick with a slight pain in his chest. Moriko got everything she needed and took off Akio's bandage. She was shocked to see that it was nearly healed, and asked Akio what was in the jar with such healing powers. Akio explained that the Shaolin monks gave him the jar after he received his mark of the Black Dragon and told Moriko that it had healed in three days, as monks had told him. They said that it would help him heal with any future injuries that he may receive. Moriko noticed that there was one small lesion that was still weeping puss; the salve was working, as it drew out the poison from his arm. The salve was truly a miracle of medicine; she needed to try and find all its properties so she could make more for the future.

The clan was getting ready for war with the outlaw clan. Sixty-three men and women were sharpening their weapons and gathering all their equipment. They would travel at night, and hide and rest during the day; there would be no campfires from the time they left the village. This was going to be one of the largest battles that the clan could remember in twenty-three years. It was good that they set boundaries every fifty years or so; it kept peace in the region.

On the third day, Akio and Moriko were ready, as he had said; his arm had healed with little scaring from his wounds. His arm felt a little stiff, but it would be better with some use. They joined the clan and waited for the Elder to lead the way. There was one horse for the Elder, and one cart that carried provisions and medicine with some extra weapons. Akio and Moriko walked next to the Elder's horse, along with twelve archers who led the way. There were two men that carried the banner of the Iga clan; it was customary when traveling through the different regions. The Elder had a plan to see the magistrate first; to see his reaction, before he met with the Amura outlaw clan.

After three nights of traveling, the Elder decided to see the magistrate with only six men; four archers and two that carried the banners. It was not a show of force, but he wanted to make a point that he was still alive. He told the rest of the clan to slowly make their way in and around the village and make notes of the men and any fortifications and weapons. The next morning, the Elder traveled on the road, with his men, into the village of the magistrate. Some of the villagers ran away from them and alerted others that the Iga clan had entered the village. It was clearly not an attack, but more of a formal visit. A small group of soldiers blocked the entrance to the courtyard where he would have been received by the magistrate, saying that he was away on business. The Elder said that he understood, and that he was just passing by. He wanted to show his respect before going on to see the Amura Clan, the magistrate's cousin. The soldiers look of surprise said it all; as they nodded and held their ground knowing that the magistrate was hiding and watching. The Elder told his small group to turn around; they had a long way to travel. As they turned towards the road, he knew that the ruse had worked, to get people moving to warn Amura's outlaw clan.

When the Elder reached the forest, Moriko met him with three of the archers saying that they killed four of the magistrate's runners; two of them were Amura's men. Several others came in with reports of the village. There were twenty soldiers, ten horses, four lookout towers with archers, and six of Amura's men inside the main house with the magistrate. Moriko looked to see if Akio had returned from his scouting inside the village. He had not returned, but she was not worried because the Black Dragon could take care of himself and he was a master of deception and misdirection.

The Iga clan did not have time to waste by waiting for Akio. They started their journey down the road, at a rather quick pace, to get to Amura's camp just before dark. The Iga clan readied themselves for a night of fighting; they spread out in the dark and waited for the signal from their Elder. They watched as a few of the farmers, carrying baskets, entered through the gate. Moriko watched and noticed that one of them had a familiar walk and favored his right arm; it was Akio making his way to be the first inside. Moriko told the Elder that Akio was inside the camp and he would send the signal to attack. The Elder did not know how Akio had made up so much time and distance.

Amura stood over a table with three others, going over plans to wipe out the Iga clan and have the magistrate cover for them; the Yakuza had paid a high price to keep their name out of it. They wanted the Black Dragon, and the Iga clan was harboring him. Akio was watching them from a small opening from the roof. He had seen enough and knew that he may have been responsible for the attack on the Iga clan. It was time for the Black Dragon to bring justice for the clan. Akio silently jumped down from the roof to the front doorway; there were no guards at the door, so he entered. Amura turned to see the Black Dragon throw metal stars into the soft tissue of the throats of the men that stood at the table. Amura grabbed a knife from his waist, but the Black Dragon had already moved. A metal star hit him in the arm and hand. The Black Dragon was not a myth; the Yakuza had reason to fear him. He moved so fast that, to the eye, he was just a blur. Amura felt the cold steel of a blade enter his chest and looked down to see his own blood before he fell to the floor dead. Akio reached inside of his robe, pulled out a small rocket and lit it from the doorway. The rocket lit up the night sky and drew everyone's attention; the signal had been sent and the attack was starting. The archers from the forest sent their arrows into the four lookout towers and killed the sentries. The Iga ninjas were climbing over the walls and the opened gates, which allowed the Elder to enter by riding on horseback to the main house. Moriko ran, as she kept pace with the Elder on horseback, and was at the door before he could dismount. They both entered the house, only to see dead bodies on the floor; Amura being one of them. Within a few minutes, the fighting was over; only some women and children were left to tell the tale of the Black Dragon. The Elder stood over the table and showed the plans. He was speechless, and knew that every man, woman, and child would have been killed. Akio stepped into the house and told them that he had made it look like the magistrate had been killed by one of Amura's men over money that the Yakuza had paid, before he left the village. He took a horse and rode to catch up, but arrived early. So, he went into the fields posed as a farmer. Akio assured him that nothing would come back to the Iga clan. The Elder looked at Akio and said, "Who said you have no powers," as he walked out the door. Akio told Moriko that her training must be finished soon. There was a sense of urgency in his voice, as they walked out and followed the clan into the forest.

The clan had been back in the mountains for several weeks, and there was no word of the battle that had taken place at the Amura stronghold. Moriko continued her training with Akio by tying the bands to her legs and wrist with Akio, as they did the moves of the Dragon. It was time for Moriko to try and put together the moves of the Dragon. Akio took her to the training yard and blind- folded her. He told her to see in her mind's eye, and to follow the moves. Akio asked four of the clan to participate in the test and try their best to hit Moriko. Moriko stood in the center of the yard and started her kata of the Dragon; she moved like a snake and then turned her head around to the sound of breathing. She kicked out and made contact and then turned again, spinning and hitting another with her fist. Two others attacked and did not see her foot come around and hit them. Akio entered the circle, spun in a small circle, and jumped into the air above Moriko. She was ready. She spun in a circle, jumped into the air and kicked Akio in midair, knocking him to the ground. Moriko had mastered the Dragons Tail, a feat that was not to be taken lightly. Moriko stood as she moved her body from side to side, twisting and turning as if she had no bones in her body. It was so memorizing that the clan members just stood and watched. Akio walked up to her and placed his hand over his fist and bowed giving respect to the new Black Dragon of the clan. Moriko stood still and took off her blindfold. She saw the members of her clan bowing in respect.

Akio held her hand and asked, "Would you accept the mark of the Dragon?" Moriko looked down at her chest and said, "Is there no other way? I would give my life for the honor, but not across my breasts." Akio understood, and told her that he had made some arrangements with the local blacksmith. They walked together, to the shop of the blacksmith, where she saw an iron in the coals of the fire; it was in the shape of a dragon. If you accept, it will be placed between your shoulder blades to be hidden by your hair. The blacksmith was ready to place the dragon to her back. Moriko said, "I accept the dragon and all it represents. I will fight for justice." Moriko felt the heat go through her and into her lungs as she screamed. Akio held her up, and put the salve, from the porcelain jar, on her burn. She did not feel the pain; instead, it was almost cold. Akio put a bandage over the area of the burn and said, "I will put this on you, for the next three days."

The next three days were not painful for Moriko. The burn healed and a perfect dragon appeared between her shoulders. She was thrilled that it looked so good. At the same time, she knew that only her clan would know about her training to be the next Black Dragon. Akio sat with Moriko and the Elder. He had some bad news to share with them. The Elder had tea for them, as they sat in a small area known for meditation. Moriko asked, "What is it you need to share with us? Are you leaving us?" Akio looked at her and said, "I will always be with you. We are family; this clan is family, but I am dying. I have passed on my knowledge to you and the clan; guard it well and tell Haruto and Aoi that they have responsibility to bring justice and pass on their knowledge to the next generation, until we have found justice from the Yakuza." The Elder nodded in agreement, and was saddened at the news. Akio explained that the poison from his wound had reached his heart and although the wound healed, the damage had been done. He would only have a few months left and wanted the Elder to know how thankful he was that his family had been in such good hands with the Iga clan. Moriko had tears running down her face and the Elder comforted her. The Elder asked, "What can we do to make your passing easier?" Akio said, "I would like to continue training the clan members, but have shorter training periods. Nothing else gives me more pleasure than to spread the teachings of the Shaolin." The Elder nodded his head and agreed.

Akio walked away from the meditation room and told Moriko that he had a special request of her. Moriko was eager to do anything he requested and said, "I will do anything requested of my father." "I would like you to join me as one, and make one last visit to the Yakuza in the last days of the Dragon Festival," replied Akio. Moriko had just realized that another year was passing soon, and it would be time for the Black Dragon to make a visit to the Yakuza; which meant traveling into the city.

The next few months of training was harder than the previous training she had received. She had bands on her ankles and wrists and was blindfolded with Akio. They used several weapons; they always moved as one, which made it difficult to tell them apart. They were faster and stronger; the Dragon kata made more sense now and became second nature. During the last few weeks of training, they dressed the same; in black, tight clothing with black hoods and had their weapons inside their boots and up their sleeves. They were as one, and it was time to make a visit to the city. Moriko and Akio told the Elder that they were going into the city for several days and would be back as soon as possible. The Elder knew it was the time of the Dragon Festival.

The next day, they traveled on the road and pulled a cart of goods to trade in the city. If anyone had seen or stopped them, they looked to pose no threat; just farmers traveling to the city. Once in the city, they stopped at several restaurants and asked the owners or cooks if they needed any fresh vegetables for the day. The plan was clever. Posing as farmers, all the while getting information on the clientele and finding the headquarters of the Yakuza. By midday, they had found the bathhouse and headquarters of the Yakuza that ran half of the city. They watched and counted all the men that went in and out of the bathhouse, and made mental notes of the two-story building that was their headquarters. At the end of the day, they walked out of the city and pushed the empty cart into a field near the road; it was time to plan. Akio wanted to make sure that they were not going to fail. They were going to enter from the roof into the bathhouse and kill all those that had the markings of the Yakuza. It was easy, as they were the ones with all the tattoos. Moriko asked, "Are we going separately first, or going in as one?" Akio looked somewhat surprised; it was a good question. "We will go in as one, and move as the Black Dragon will lead us," replied Akio. It was good because she had never done anything like this except in training; she would follow her instincts. It was near midnight, when Akio and Moriko reached the bathhouse. They were on the roof, and at last count, there were nearly thirty men inside. Akio started to remove the tiles on the roof to make an opening large enough for them to jump down. Nobody noticed the stars showing through the roof, as there was just large plumes of steam coming off the bath waters. They came down into the corner of the room between two men sitting with towels over their heads. They did not even bother to look up; they just moved over enough so that another person could sit down. Moriko put a knife into the back of their skulls, and they died where they sat. The Dragon moved on to the next target, just five feet away. A short man was sitting on the edge of the pool. He felt a slight breeze, as he looked up to see a short sword moving across his throat; he slipped into the water turning it crimson. There was a group of men in the water at the end of the pool. Walking along the pool would bring attention to them, so they jumped into the pool next to them. It startled them and they started to yell and move away from the black figure; the Black Dragon spun with blades out, and cut down the men where they stood, one falling into the water. Blood was everywhere on the floor and in the pool. Another group of men heard the splashing and saw that there were dead bodies in the water. They ran toward the dark figure. The man leading the group, slipped and fell from all the blood that was on the floor; it started being a domino effect with the rest of the men, who slipped in the blood and fell. The Black Dragon found them easy prey and killed them as they tried to stand up and run in the opposite direction. There were some men coming out of a room half dressed with swords or a knife in hand. There was not much room for them to maneuver, due to the number of pools that were in the bathhouse. They were all in a line, staying on the walkways in between the pools. It was easy for the Black Dragon to jump from side to side, and kill the men, as they jumped across to the next pool. There were multiple dead bodies in the pools that were floating half-submerged, with deep cuts along their bodies; some without limbs or heads. Along the pool's walkways, there were half-nude bodies covered in blood; all the men inside were dead. This normally would been enough for the Black Dragon to send a loud and clear message, but the opportunity was too easy with their headquarters being next door. There had been no yelling or cries for help. There were no alarms and nobody escaped. This attack went perfectly.

The two-story building was quiet and only one room was lit by a candle on the second floor. A guard stood in the doorway; it looked like a trap. Akio asked Moriko, "What do you think and what do you feel?" "I think it may be a trap, it does not feel right. Why would there be thirty plus men next to a building that is their headquarters, with only one man as a look out, unless he is bait?" replied Moriko. "We must find who is really watching from a distance. Let us split up and hunt these men; they would not be ready for two Black Dragons." said Akio. The next two-story warehouse building, three doors down. It was a good place to start looking. They both stayed in the shadows and out of sight, as they worked their way around the building. They both heard a sound coming from the roof at the same time. They both climbed the opposite building, next to the warehouse, and went to the rear to try and get a better vantage of the sound. What they saw shocked them; there were at least twenty ninjas with bows and arrows lying in wait, watching the building. Moriko and Akio took out a small pouch and a bamboo tube. They would dart as many as they could, and use their throwing stars to finish them. They started from the ends and worked their way to the middle; there were no sounds, as the ninjas were being picked off, one at a time. Akio threw two stars and killed all but one who was in the center of the group. Moriko and Akio both spun and leaped into the air, both landing next to the survivor with their swords next to his throat. The ninja was shocked to see two Black Dragons next to him, and saw that all the others were not moving. Akio disarmed him and took off his black head covering. This was not a ninja. He was a paid mercenary who was hired by the Yakuza. Akio asked him, "How many are there?" The ninja smiled and said, "Hundreds". Akio slit his throat without any hesitation. Moriko asked, "What are we going to do?" We are going to burn them out. Akio told Moriko to quickly gather all the arrows from the dead ninjas with two bows. Akio took some of the clothes from the ninjas and made rags. Moriko wrapped the rags around the arrows, while Akio left and came back with lamp oil. They were ready within a few minutes to start the building on fire. They shot several arrows on each side of the building, near the bottom, so the fire would go up the walls. They waited until the men started to come out. At first, there was smoke and then fire. This created a lot of confusion; the people inside were yelling and screaming, as they rushed to open the door, to be met with arrows to the chest. The Black Dragon had run out of arrows sooner than they expected, and the bodies of the dead were blocking a fast exit. The fire got hotter and bigger and those inside became desperate, as they pushed and shoved others in front of them, to exit. The Black Dragon jumped from the roof spinning with their blades out on both sides of the doorway, cutting down those that dared to exit. The Black Dragon had to step into the street due to the heat of the fire. They watched as the roof fell in and the walls started to collapse. The fire had awakened many of the people who lived in the area, who started to yell for help to put out the fire before other buildings burned to the ground. People even tried to bring water to the fire, but it was hopeless; in all the smoke and confusion, the Black Dragon melted into the shadows as they left the city.

As Akio and Moriko walked along the road, they saw their cart still in the field where they left it. They pulled it back onto the road to travel back to their village, posing as farmers. In the weeks that followed, news came from the city stating that the Black Dragon had killed over a hundred Yakuza and burned their headquarters to the ground in the last days of the Dragon Festival. The city had runners post reward signs in the surrounding villages, with a bounty for information leading to the arrest of the Black Dragon; the money was put up by the Yakuza. The magistrate called in the Army to find and arrest the Black Dragon. So, the stories grew into the legend of the Black Dragon. Every year at the time of the Dragon Festival, the Yakuza would try to hide from the Black Dragon; and every year, the Black Dragon would find two or three of them and bring justice.

Akio died with the Iga clan around him, two months after he returned to the village. His body was burned and his ashes were buried under the temple shrine of the Iga clan. Moriko was saddened and was not sure how to notify Haruto, or even if she should. So, she asked for guidance from the Elder of the clan. His words were simple after much thought. He said, "The clan has lost a great teacher and he will be missed for generations, but he has left us with a legacy to fight for justice." Moriko thought about her husband and Aoi. They were still training with the Shaolin in China. When would they return? It was a question that was answered ten years later, with their return to the Iga clan. Moriko was now almost forty and the clan Elder had passed away years ago; now lying next to Akio. The new Elder, Arakawa, was wise and split up the clan into small cells that could stay in touch with runners or fires from the towers. The Elder was a master of strategies and knew his enemies. The training of the clan was paramount; they were the Iga ninja; the best that Japan had ever seen and were becoming one of the largest.

The return of Haruto and Aoi was filled with joy, but the news of Akio and the Elder had dampened the mood. The village clan people were happy to be as one family again; training and following the ways of the Dragon. Haruto showed the scar of the Black Dragon on his chest and gave her a small porcelain jar with the salve and instructions on how to make it; it would be a family secret to be passed on for generations. Haruto and Moriko shared the knowledge of the Black Dragon and Moriko showed the scar on her back. Now, they could be as one. Moriko had gone to other cities, over the last ten years, looking for the Yakuza and bringing justice with her. Haruto was proud that she was able to carry on as the Black Dragon, and now they could join forces. Aoi was seventeen and she was tasked to be the new training assistant to the Iga clan. She still had much to learn about her Iga ninja clan and the ways they fought. Aoi was very mature for her age. She was stubborn and trained harder than anyone close to her age. She was perfect in her form and choice of weapons for the desired outcome. Aoi would become one of the greatest warriors of the clan, in the years to come; it was her destiny. Aoi cared for Moriko. She had fallen ill with the flu; a sickness that swept through Japan, with a vengeance, killing hundreds. Even the Emperor was sick. Aoi was now helping others in the village. She was always looking to be of help in the fields or in training. It did not matter what she did, because she was selfless; cooking and washing clothes was not beneath her. The Iga clan loved her for her strength and stubbornness. There was only one man that dared to call on her in all the years that she was with the clan. He was Kenji Arakawa the Elder's youngest, twenty-eight year old son . He had been trained most of his life by Aoi and he practiced his skills at night; on a regular schedule after his duties and chores were done. To call on Aoi Katsumi, had to be well thought out. He was smitten with her beauty and strength; she was very knowledgeable as a warrior and a natural born leader; what was not to love. At first, Aoi did not respond to his advances; even if they were very slight. But, he was persistent and was very handsome. Moriko was dying. Aoi had been helping to fight her high fever for a week and she was getting weaker; even after drinking her tea remedies. Nothing seemed to help. Aoi was by her side, day and night. Haruto was with her, as he tried to help her care for her mother. They tried to keep her fever down and keep her comfortable by wiping her down and covering her. Aoi held her hand while Moriko spoke softly, asking her to ensure their legacy and to find a husband. Aoi told her that there would be plenty of time for such things. Moriko pressed the issue and had her promise to bring justice to their family. Aoi had promised Moriko; she smiled and closed her eyes for the last time. Haruto and the Iga clan suffered a crushing blow with the death of Moriko. The clan mourned her death and laid her to rest at the temple. Aoi took her death hard. She trained the clan warriors harder and pushed them to the breaking point; if she could train hard, so could they. Haruto took Aoi aside and talked to her as the Elder Arakawa listened. Aoi explained that if she failed in her duties to the clan, they would all die at the hands of their enemies. Haruto told her to remember her training with the Shaolin and follow a gentle, but strong, path to a greater purpose in life, other than to one's own interest. Aoi lowered her head and felt shame for not knowing how to express her feelings. She missed her mother and grandfather. She had not trained to respond to the death of family members. The Elder Arakawa took Aoi in his arms and held her saying, "You have not been a child for a long time. It is time you weep and take time to honor your family and heal your heart." Haruto had never seen or heard of an Elder understand a young woman's heart. He was a good leader and father to the clan.

Time had passed and with time, Aoi healed. But she missed her mother just the same, and her father had taken responsibility for all the training for the clan. Aoi had started doing things that she never had time to do, like fishing; it was one of grandfather's favorite pastimes. Kenji had seen her fishing several times and finally asked if he could join her. He was surprised that she accepted so fast. They had fun catching fish and taking long walks; which was not very common in the clan. Aoi had her conditions. Kenji had to agree to train with her at night. Kenji agreed, since he was already training at night. Haruto had seen her at night, walking to the training yard with a staff or a bow. When he saw Kenji while training, he was going to ask her when she would be ready to take over the training program. Aoi was fulfilling her promise to her mother and it pleased him that she had been able to see her path.

5

GOING FISHING

HARUTO JOINED ELDER Arakawa near the temple to watch Aoi and Kenji training alone, and saw them training harder and faster; switching off styles from the Shaolin to the Iga ninja. Kenji has gotten better by training with Aoi. Elder Arakawa asked Haruto, "When are you going to start Aoi in the Black Dragon ways? She is ready." Haruto nodded in agreement saying, "Her heart is going to choose her path and she will fulfill her destiny." The Elder smiled and said, "I believe we will have a wedding soon; they are inseparable. The Dragon Festival is coming soon. Will you be traveling to the city?" Haruto replied, "I will be going to the docks this time; the Yakuza control the shipping wherever they go. They can control a country by buying its shipping and they already have too much influence in the government. I will be traveling alone and I will be leaving soon to formulate my plan. The legend of the Black Dragon has always put the city magistrate on edge and he uses soldiers to look for all strangers that visit."

Aoi and Kenji had finished their training and sat opposite each other, resting in silence and listening to their surroundings. Aoi looked at Kenji and motioned with her eyes towards the temple. Kenji smiled; he also heard footsteps from the temple. There was a very slight nod from Kenji and he slowly got up and turned towards the temple steps and bowed towards his father. Elder Arakawa smiled, as did Haruto. Aoi got up, turned and bowed. Kenji would ask for her hand at the next full moon.

Haruto left for the city the next day, and told Aoi to take over the training until his return. It was time for the Black Dragon to pay a visit to the Yakuza. His father had left the city of Akita for China; it had grown as well as the fishing docks. It would be interesting to see the docks. He would have to blend in enough as a fisherman, to not bring attention to himself. The Yakuza had many spies, as well as the soldiers, to contend with all the time. They checked everyone during the time of the Dragon Festival. Haruto had an old knife that his father used when fishing, and carried it in his waistband, as any normal fisherman would do.

Haruto walked into the city and along the docks without any problems. It was early morning and many men were getting ready to head out to sea. Haruto stopped several times to see if anyone needed an extra hand with the nets. There was one man who had sized him up asking if he knew how to use the knife on his waistband. Haruto nodded. The man grabbed his hands and looked at them; they were hard and calloused and then slapped his stomach. "You do not eat much," he exclaimed. "I am Daichi and I own this boat. Do you want work?" Haruto nodded. "Get on board and we will leave when my other man shows up, or I will skin him for not showing up for another day." Haruto got on board and sat near the sails while he looked over everything. Daichi yelled, "Hurry up and don't tell me you over-slept." The young man he was yelling at, was fat and breathing hard by the time he reached the boat. The man looked at Haruto and said, "I am

Tarou, who are you?" "I am Haruto. Daichi hired me to help." "I am forced to work under Daichi. My father says I need to work more and eat less." Daichi yelled to cast off the lines. Haruto did as he was told, and watched as Daichi took the rudder. They sailed out to sea. Haruto liked the sea; it felt good to him. He liked the way his legs moved with the waves. It was not long before Daichi was barking orders again to release the nets. The boat tipped to one side and Tarou's eyes grew wide. He was not expecting the boat to tip so much. He lost his balance and fell overboard. Daichi yelled at Haruto to grab Tarou. Haruto grabbed him by his hair and held his head above the water. Daichi reached over and grabbed Tarou by the arm and pulled him into the boat with Haruto's help. The boat was still tipping far on its side. "Pull up the nets," Daichi ordered, "Tarou, go sit on the side of the boat and don't move." Haruto was now using all of his strength to pull in the nets. Daichi was swearing that he never had such a catch, as the fish started pouring into the boat from the nets. There was tuna in the nets along with mackerel. They caught a school of tuna chasing the mackerel. The boat made its way back to the dock, with Daichi still barking orders to Tarou and Haruto to be ready with the rope to tie it up to the dock, and to be careful not to fall into the water again. Haruto told Tarou not to take it personal; it could have happened to anyone. Tarou said, "But, it happened to me. My father will be embarrassed." "Who is your father?" asked Haruto. "I thought everybody knew my father. He owns the docks and several boats. I hate fishing. He makes me work for Daichi saying I must learn the business of the docks," replied Tarou. "Oh, my father is Goro Takashi." Daichi told Haruto to clean up so he could meet Mr. Takashi. He will want to meet the man who saved his son's life. Haruto tried to explain, "I did no such thing; it was you that pulled him into the boat." Daichi said he would not hear of anymore nonsense as he said, "Besides, you could be paid handsomely for your quick actions." Haruto did not want the attention and thought of walking away from the docks. But doing so, might bring even more attention to him.

Daichi took Haruto to Mr. Takashi. Tarou walked behind them saying he wanted to find some dry clothes. As they entered the second-story office building overlooking the docks, Mr. Takashi sat behind a desk covered in papers. Mr. Takashi asked why his son was soaking wet? Daichi explained what happened saying it was good fortune that made him fall into the sea. The market was going to be filled with tuna that would bring a high price when sold. Mr. Takashi was not amused and told Tarou to find dry clothes. He opened a drawer and pulled out a small pouch of coins for Haruto and handed it to him saying, "You would have been paid more had he drowned." He hated the boy. "He is fat and lazy and has no stomach for the business." Haruto took the coins and bowed saying," Thank you," as he backed up and turned to leave. Mr. Takashi told Daichi that he did not know what good fortune was and told him to leave. Haruto would never forget the eyes of Mr. Takashi and the cold heart of a man who hated his own son.

Daichi walked with Haruto along the dock and put his arm around him asking, "So, are you going to buy me a drink now? After all, you would never have had those coins if it were not for me." "Sure," replied Haruto. "So, when will I be paid for today's great fortune, for all the tuna we caught?" Daichi gave him a look and said, "Come see me tomorrow night after the market closes. You will be paid then; Mr. Takashi does the payroll, so you will have a good payday. Would you consider coming out tomorrow to work? I would like to have you as a regular hand; better than that worthless Tarou.""I will see you at the docks in the morning, I need the work," replied Haruto. "Hey, what about that drink?" asked Daichi. "My stomach needs more than a drink of wine right now," said Haruto. Haruto looked for a place to eat and a boarding house in which to sleep.

Daichi watched him walk away; something was off a bit with Haruto and he could not figure it out. The guy was a good hand and he knew his way around a boat. He had the legs for it, and had good balance. Tomorrow would be another day; if he worked out, maybe he could be part of the dock enforcers. Mr. Takashi was always looking for good people to run his docks.

The restaurant that Haruto found was crowded. People had heard that a boat with a great tuna catch had docked, and they were waiting for the fresh delivery. The restaurant owner told them to be patient and started to take orders ahead of the delivery. Haruto heard the people talking and asked a man who stood in line, if he knew of a clean boarding house where he could stay while working at the docks. The man looked at him, up and down and asked if he worked for Mr. Takashi. "They have their own boarding house where all their workers stay," Haruto stated. "I am just looking for some temporary accommodations, away from the criminal element." The man nodded his head and said, "Good, there are too many criminals walking the docks and markets; you may stay at my home. I have a small room if you are traveling alone?" "Yes, I am alone. My wife passed away," said Haruto. He did not lie. "How much will you charge me? I have but a few coins today. I will be paid for my work tomorrow; I was an extra hand working on the boat that caught all the tuna today." The man bowed his head. "Thank you; it has been weeks since anyone as caught good quality tuna for the restaurants and markets. My name is Hiroshi Sato," as he bowed his head again. "I am Haruto," and bowed back to Hiroshi. Haruto waited until Hiroshi received a small package of fish and walked back to his house with him.

Along the way, Hiroshi was happy to talk to someone. He also lost his wife when all of Japan suffered due to the flu. Haruto asked about the criminal element along the docks and the markets. Hiroshi was a wealth of information; he had lived near the docks all his life. The docks were controlled by the Takashi Trading Company and owned by the

Yakuza. The markets were controlled by the Yakuza, and the magistrate of the city got paid by both, for looking the other way. Hiroshi said it had not always been that way, but time has a way of changing things. As they reached Hiroshi's house, he asked, "How long would you like to stay? No charge, if you keep things clean and can cook?" Haruto said, "I can cook and I don't drink wine. I work and can bring fish to your table." Hiroshi laughed and nodded his head saying, "I don't cook very well." Haruto laughed and said it has been a long day and he would like to eat and then sleep. Hiroshi put a pot on the small fire for tea and asked Haruto to make the fish anyway he wished. Haruto bowed his head and told Hiroshi that he would be back as soon as he got a few things for the meal and left. Haruto had seen a small market just a few doors down and brought back some vegetables and a large rice ball in a bamboo basket. The meal that Haruto made looked like a feast for the emperor. Hiroshi looked at all the food and he bowed his head saying that he was not worthy of such a meal. Haruto replied, "Nonsense, this is a simple meal, let us eat; I am starving." While they were eating, they talked about fishing and farming. Haruto knew all about these things and was happy to have good company. The talking took a turn about the injustice of living with a criminal element within the docks. The few women that were left, after the flu swept through the city, were gathered up by the Yakuza for slaves in their brothels. Hiroshi brought up the Black Dragon; the only thing that the Yakuza feared. The tales were close to the truth; all but the flying and breathing fire part. Haruto played the innocent part and stated that he had only heard of a few tales about the Black Dragon; everybody knew some of the stories, even in the countryside.

The evening ended with Haruto saying that he had to work early in the morning and went to his room. Hiroshi picked up the plates and thanked him again for the fine meal. Haruto waited until Hiroshi went to sleep before he slipped out into the city towards the docks. He stayed in the shadows and moved slowly as he watched and listened. He found what he was looking for; two blocks from the fishing dock. He heard the familiar voice of Daichi. He was sitting at a table with several other men, drinking and making a few women sit with them. The women were clearly there by force. They hated being grabbed and pawed; this was not respectful for women. One of the men grabbed a small woman by the hair and forced a kiss on her neck. When she pulled away from him, he slapped her hard across the face. Another man laughed and picked her up off the floor only to grab at her private parts and try to kiss her again. She refused his advances and was slapped across the face again, only to have the whole scene repeat itself. The woman's last act of defiance was when she bit the man's cheek. The man grabbed her by the throat and held her up off the floor against the wall and stabbed her in the chest with his knife. Daichi yelled at the man for killing her and told him to get rid of the body; women were hard to find and now Mr. Takashi would be mad for losing a source of income. The incident meant that they had to find a replacement; which meant they would have to go into the countryside again to find someone. They would have to make plans soon, and with luck, Mr. Takashi would not notice a new girl in the brothel.

As Haruto made his way back to Hiroshi's, he made a mental note of the man that killed the woman. He would be easy to find with a bite mark on his cheek. Hiroshi was still sleeping when Haruto quietly went to bed. He had dreams of finding the men responsible for all the injustice done to the people; the Black Dragon would have his day, and it was coming soon.

The morning came sooner than Haruto wanted; he was still thinking about the man with the bite mark on his cheek and the dead woman. When Haruto got to Daichi's boat, he saw a man with a bite mark on his cheek, already standing there waiting for Daichi. Haruto gave the man a nod saying, "My name is Haruto. Daichi hired me yesterday to work on his boat." The man grunted saying, "I am Buntodo," as he walked towards the stern of the boat. Haruto could clearly see that a body was rolled up in a sheet; he stayed away from the stern of the boat. Daichi came running up to the boat telling Buntodo to shove off before Tarou showed up; he did not need to have Mr. Takashi's son talking about the body. The boat was about fifty yards away when they heard Tarou yelling, "I'm on time!" Daichi laughed, and waved as the boat got farther away out to sea. Daichi put his arm around Haruto and walked him to the bow of the boat and told him that Buntodo had to get rid of some trash from the market. Haruto heard the splash of the body hitting the sea. He did not turn to look, nor would he ever forgive Buntodo or Daichi, for that matter. The Black Dragon would have his justice.

The fishing was terrible; not even close to half of what they caught yesterday. Daichi stated that it was the weather; there was a storm coming in. If he only knew that the storm was the Black Dragon, and the time was very close for him to appear to find justice. When they reached the dock, Haruto asked about his pay from yesterday. He was told to see Mr. Takashi. He was the one to see about payroll. Haruto walked to the end of the dock where Mr. Takashi's office looked over the dock. He could see him standing in the window looking out at the sea. Haruto walked up the steps and knocked on the door. Tarou opened the door. Haruto saw that Tarou had a red, swollen face from being slapped repeatedly. Mr. Takashi turned to see Haruto standing in front of his desk and asked, "How long do you plan on staying here? I control the docks and who works here. I do not know you. Where do you come from?" Haruto looked at Mr. Takashi and said, "I took some day work fishing with Daichi. He said you might be able to use a man like me on your docks." Mr. Takashi walked around Haruto and looked at him and asked, "I will not ask you again. Where do you come from?" This time, he pulled out a samurai sword and laid it on the shoulders of Haruto. Haruto replied, "Sir, please, I meant no disrespect. I come from a small village near the mountains. My wife died from the flu and our fields failed this year. Our village is starving and I promised to bring food from the city." Mr. Takashi saw that he was trembling with fear and said, "You are weak and I don't need weak men working for me. Take your wages and leave the docks or I will have Daichi feed you to the fish." Mr. Takashi opened his desk drawer and took out a small bag of coins, not much bigger than yesterdays coins, and said that he took out his fees for working for him without a permit. Haruto took the coins as he backed up and bowed, saying thank you, as he left the office.

Haruto walked to the fishing boat and saw Daichi and tossed him a coin saying, "Here is your drink money. I have been ordered to leave the docks by Mr. Takashi. Would it be alright if I could take one fish for dinner tonight?" Daichi told him, "Take two fish; Mr. Takashi is a hard man to deal with sometimes." The walk to Hiroshi's house was with purpose. The Black Dragon was needed tonight and he had to prepare. Haruto had to make another dinner fit for an emperor, but this time he had to ensure that Hiroshi slept well and long. The dinner was without flaws and Hiroshi was very happy that Haruto knew how to cook. Haruto served him some tea and told him it was a special blend to calm him and make him sleep better. Hiroshi told him that he had no trouble sleeping, and he had no troubles. Haruto nodded saying, "Just being thoughtful." Hiroshi told him that he must have made his wife very happy. Haruto smiled saying that he missed her very much and had to fulfill a promise. Sleep well, my friend, as he watched Hiroshi fall asleep at the table.

The three drops of sleeping potion in the tea did the trick; Hiroshi would sleep all night. Haruto went into his room and unrolled his black clothing and hood and was able to blend into the night. He needed to find a few weapons and knifes, but did not think that would be a problem with such a large criminal element at the docks. He knew of a very fine sword in an office overlooking the docks and he would be happy to relieve it from Mr. Takashi, along with his head. Tarou would be free from the tyrant.

The Black Dragon was on the move and was already looking at the office of Mr. Takashi. It was near midnight and the office was lit up and there were guards standing around talking. They were Yakuza. The door of the office opened and Tarou came out, falling down the steps; he had been thrown out after being beaten by his father. One of the men laughed and kicked him, telling him to leave the area before his father changed his mind and killed him. Tarou limped away into the darkness crying, and saying that he hated his father.

The Black Dragon took out his fishing knife and made his way within a few feet of the guards. He stayed in the shadows, while he made a scraping noise on the wood and got the attention of two guards. They tried to investigate the shadows, but were met with a knife across their throats. They were dragged into the darkness away from the light. A scraping sound again, brought another guard, but this time he took out his sword and told anyone in the shadow to come out. A knife came out of the darkness and hit soft tissue at the bottom of the throat; he died unable to make a sound for help. There was a guard at the top of the stairs, by the door to the office. The Black Dragon climbed the stairs, upside down, to where the guard was standing and cut his Achilles tendons with one stroke. The man fell on the porch and saw a black figure as it moved fast and out of sight. The last thing he felt was a knife being driven into the back of his skull. The office door opened with a man falling over the dead body; he was cussing and tried to draw his sword, but he was too late. The Black Dragon put a knife through the man's eye, killing him instantly. The Black Dragon jumped through the doorway and avoided a man who was hiding behind the door, as he tried to stab him. The Black Dragon was in a very low, crouching stance looking at the three people in the room. They knew it was the Black Dragon. He had come for them and they knew it, as they all had their swords at the ready. They were going to kill this Black Dragon once and for all; he was a man, not a myth or fairy tale, and he could die. A moment of silence was in the room just before they heard, "I will dance in your blood and stand on your bones before I die." The men rushed him. The Black Dragon was no longer in the same spot. He had jumped on the desk and kicked one man as he took his sword from him; turned him around and shoved him into the others who held their swords. He was impaled by his own men. The Black Dragon spun in a small circle and kicked up blood from the dead man. Mr. Takashi was slashing at the air, trying to make contact and missing; instead, he cut his partner across his arm. Mr. Takashi moved around, trying not to be the next dead man, as he saw his partner being cut multiple times across the chest and face. His sword hit the floor and was no longer of use to him. He was dying on his feet bleeding out. The Black Dragon focused his attention on Takashi wanting him to realize that justice had found him. He hit the sword hand of Takashi, making him drop his sword. The blow did not cut him, as he looked down to see his hand. The Black Dragon put his foot underneath the sword with his foot, and kicked it in the air as he caught it. Looking at the sword, he saw that it was of great value. "How did you come across such a fine and well-made Hanzo sword? I will not ask you again." Mr. Takashi looked down and was about to speak when the sword blade rested on his shoulder, next to his neck. Takashi looked up with his eyes wide saying, "I know who…" The sword went across his neck with one swift movement and his head rolled off his body onto the floor, followed by his body. Mr. Takashi never got to finish his last thought. Tarou was now free from his tyrant father; a Yakuza crime lord of the docks.

The Black Dragon was not finished that night. He went in search of Daichi and Buntodo and he knew just where to find them. The boarding house and the brothels were not far from the docks. He slipped into the shadows again, waiting and listening with the Hanzo sword in hand. The familiar voice of Daichi was near; he was drunk, and had a woman by the arm, dragging her into the dark alley. The shadows favored the Black Dragon who was nearly invisible to the eye. Daichi hit the woman with his fist knocking her out. As she lay there unconscious, Daichi pulled down his pants. A voice from the dark said, "Justice is here for you, Daichi." The sword came down fast; not even slowing, as it went through bone and tissue, the blade so sharp it cut Daichi in half. The Black Dragon picked up the woman and took her to a nearby home and put her in the doorway, away from the dead body. It was time to find Buntodo. The search did not take long, as he was in the bar pawing at a woman. Other men were laughing at his advances, seeing how the woman was very old and tired. There were seven men in the bar and only three old women to see to their needs; all the young women were missing. The Black Dragon entered the bar from the rear. Nobody noticed him standing in the shadows. It took only a few seconds to formulate a plan to bring justice to them, but he wanted Buntodo to know it was his time to answer for the death of an innocent woman. An old woman disappeared behind the bar and she called out asking for another woman to help her move a barrel of wine. The woman that Buntodo was with, quickly moved away towards the bar, which pissed off Buntodo as he slammed his fist down on the table. The rest of the men laughed harder at Buntodo and said that the only way he was going to have sex was if he killed her first. Buntodo was mad now, as he got up and turned the table over and moved towards the bar; only to be met by the Black Dragon standing in front of him. The other men saw the Black Dragon standing in the same room and stood up to draw their swords. Buntodo was too drunk to understand what was happening, as the words were heard by the group, that justice would be served. The head of Buntodo was cut in half; the sword followed through to mid-chest before the blade was drawn out of the body. The men screamed like frightened children and dropped their swords on the floor as they tried to run out the door. They did not make it. The Black Dragon cut them down like dry wheat; it was over in a few seconds. The Black Dragon grabbed a cloth towel from the bar area and cleaned the blood off the Hanzo sword. It was one of the finest swords ever made. How Mr. Takashi found such a prize item, he will never know now, but he will put it to good use. As the Black Dragon walked out the door, he saw two men running towards him with swords in hand; they were no match and they were also cut down. The bodies of the dead were starting to pile up, in and around the bar. The night was still young, so the Black Dragon looked for the next bar with Yakuza; the criminal element was thick along the docks.

In the early hours of dawn, the sky was red and the Black Dragon had blood of others all over his clothing. It was time to leave the city docks and let the city magistrate sort out the mess. In the hours that followed, a hundred soldiers had entered the streets along the docks, and found body parts. They followed the trail of blood, which only led to more dead bodies. Many of the soldiers got sick to their stomachs and vomited in the street; they had never seen such death in the manner that it was dealt.

6

AFTERMATH

THE BODIES OF the dead were nearly cut in half at a diagonal angle; either from left to right or right to left, from the neck to under the arm. Sometimes the heads were cut in half to the shoulder or the arms had been cut off above the elbow. It was hard to fathom that a single cut from a sword could do that, but the bodies of the dead showed that this was indeed the case. The soldiers called that night's incident; the Fury of the Black Dragon. Many who lived in the area never heard the screams of the men dying. Only the criminal element was left lying in the streets; not a single innocent person was harmed. It would be hard for the magistrate to explain this to the Emperor, if he were to inquire about this incident. The Black Dragon had disappeared again. They would have to wait for another year before he showed up again. Knowing where he will show up, was the key; he never hit the same area twice. The body count was near one hundred and the stories of those killed by the Black Dragon were already growing larger in the city.

Haruto walked in the shadows until he found a bathhouse and slipped in to bathe himself; he had to rid himself of the smell. His clothes were already turning stiff from the blood that had soaked them. While he was cleaning himself, pouring water over his head, he felt that eyes were watching him. He looked around and saw nothing. He finished and got out of the water when he saw a small pair of feet sticking out from a curtain near the towel rack. He made like he did not see anything and put a towel around himself before he reached in and grabbed a small arm; it was a very young girl. The girl put both hands over her eyes and said, "I'm sorry, I didn't see anything." Haruto replied, "There is nothing to see, I am but a man wanting a bath and some clean clothes." The small girl said that she was put in charge until her mother returned from working near the docks; she works hard to feed us. Haruto smiled saying, "It is hard work to be a mother. Could you find me some clean clothes?" The girl smiled and said, "I have some fresh clothes that haven't been picked up in two days. I will be right back," as she bowed her head and ran to get the clothes. Haruto took the curtain down and wrapped the sword. He took his clothes and put them in a pile. When the girl returned, he gave her instructions not to wash the clothes, but to burn them. The girl nodded her head and took the clothes away. Haruto put the clothes on, and saw that the clothes were that of a wealthy man; the material was of a fine quality and the stitching was tight and well made. These clothes would help him walk out of the city unnoticed; except for the sword. He would have to hide it under his robe.

In the days that followed, rumors and stories were told about that night; the Fury of the Black Dragon; the rivers of blood and the deaths of hundreds. Haruto smiled to himself knowing the truth. The Yakuza never returned to those docks. That part of the City of Akita was free from the criminals that ran the docks. Justice had been served. A boy by the name of Tarou Takashi walked the docks. He was not his father; as he would do his best to keep the docks free from the Yakuza.

He was now the owner of several fishing boats and buildings, and he had inherited more money than he had ever seen. In the years that followed, he kept the docks free and had opened new restaurants and markets during the time of the Dragon Festival. He had red flags with the Black Dragon symbol fly over all of his buildings.

It was time for Haruto to train his daughter as the Black Dragon. She was ready, physically and mentally. Aoi would marry soon and she would have other things on her mind besides training. She could be ready by the next Dragon Festival. All things considered, a move to another part of Japan might be in order; the Iga clan was safe and well trained. It was time to move and there would be other hunting grounds. The Yakuza were all over Japan.

When Haruto walked into the village, it was peaceful and quiet; the sun was just coming up over the mountains. Aoi and Kenji were walking into the village from fishing when they saw Haruto. Aoi handed the fish to Kenji and ran to her father and stopped and bowed in front of him, before hugging him. She asked if he had been hurt. Haruto smiled and held her; she was happy again and he could tell that she had more than a hug on her mind. Kenji bowed and told Haruto that he was missed and he was happy to see that his business in the city went well. "We have so much to talk about, maybe after tea?" asked Kenji. "That would be fine, and have your father there also, I would like to talk to him," replied Haruto. Kenji smiled and bowed saying, "Of course, it would be my honor." Kenji knew that Haruto had already figured it out that he was going to ask for Aoi's hand. Kenji and Aoi set up the tea ceremony and had four seats at the table; it was a very serious affair, and not to be taken lightly. Everybody had to be dressed in proper attire and Aoi would be serving the tea.

Elder Arakawa was seated first, that afternoon, and Haruto Katsumi was next with an empty seat for Aoi next to him. Kenji sat next to his father and they all bowed as the tea was served by Aoi.

Kenji's jaw nearly hit the table; he had never seen Aoi in a formal kimono and she was stunning, to say the least. She had her hair up and set in a traditional style for a formal tea ceremony. Haruto and Elder Arakawa also had raised eyebrows; they had never seen such a beautiful woman within their clan. Haruto told Arakawa that she took after her mother; she was also beautiful and stubborn. As the small talk ended, Kenji requested to speak to Haruto about taking Aoi to be his wife. Elder Arakawa nodded and asked him why he thinks that he is ready for marriage, as did Haruto. Aoi and Keji both spoke at the same time, saying, "We love each other and we are of age to make the decision that would benefit the Iga clan." Haruto nodded and said, "You both have my blessing, on one condition." Aoi and Kenji both looked at each other and agreed. "Whatever the condition, we will do it with honor." Elder Arakawa spoke and said, "As parents, we have already had this discussion." Haruto told them that they would have to train as one, to be the next in line to be the Black Dragon and at the end of their training, if they were successful, they could be married.

Everyone agreed and were satisfied.

Aoi and Kenji sat in the dark, talking across from each other with their staffs and other weapons. This was a test for them to be able to understand the kata of the Dragon and its powers. Aoi told Kenji about the teachings of the Shaolin. She explained how she had been ready for her father to teach her the ways of the Dragon. Her mother had become the Black Dragon and had the mark in between her shoulders. She wanted to carry on the legacy and the knowledge; it was time for her, but now she had to teach everything to Kenji, so they could be one in marriage and as the Black Dragon. Kenji told her he was also ready to be one with her forever.

The training was harder than expected because Haruto was not easy on them. He gave them the bands to put around their feet and wrists and blind folded them. They trained at night, in the dark.

Together, they tried to get the right sequences to blend into each other. It was in the third week, that they were able to move together as one; without talking, they looked like different animals and moved in ways not thought possible for the human body. Haruto saw them move like the Dragon, and then like a snake. Suddenly, they started to spin in a tight circle and jumped into the air kicking a leg out; it was the Dragon's Tail. Haruto made a sound and attacked them from the front and was kicked in the chest for his efforts. Again, he jumped up and was met with the Dragon's Tail, hitting him hard. Haruto tried several more times, and each time he was repelled. He was getting nowhere. Haruto took out the Hanzo sword and swung it through the air, making a swishing sound. He stood ready to attack them. Aoi and Kenji were as one, as they were in a snake style kata; moving slowly from side to side, and then, without warning, they jumped into the air above Haruto. The feet of the Dragon hit Haruto on the top of his head and then on the back of his head. Haruto fell forward to the ground and dropped the sword. Haruto was slow to move; he was alive, but hurting. His head was ringing loudly and he thought he had lost some teeth. Haruto looked up to see the Dragon in a style he had never seen before. Aoi had been keeping secrets taught to her by the Shaolin. Haruto clapped his hands and Aoi and Kenji lowered their heads and put their hands together; hand over fist. They had surpassed all expectations and a new movement had been added to the Black Dragon. Haruto told them that they had passed the test and they could marry. Kenji and Aoi hugged each other and then bowed their heads. Haruto asked them if they would be willing to take the mark of the Black Dragon? If so, they could do so in a day after the wedding. They both agreed and Aoi asked if she could take the mark as her mother did? Between the shoulder blades. Haruto nodded and said that this would be a good way to honor her mother. Kenji asked if he could take the same brand, but on his chest over his heart? Haruto said, "You are now as one, so be it. I will tell the blacksmith to prepare the iron in three days." Before Kenji left with

Aoi, he asked Haruto, "Could I please hold the sword that whispered in the air?" Haruto nodded, handed the sword to him, and told him that it had unknown powers. Kenji held the sword and smiled; it was well-balanced, extremely sharp, and it felt good in his hands. He took several fighting stances with the sword, as he moved back and forth. Haruto noticed that he was a natural with the sword, and he moved with effortless skill. Kenji stopped and lowered his head and thanked Haruto as he gave him back the sword.

The wedding was set in two days time. The whole clan was preparing for the wedding; food was being gathered and the grounds of the temple were swept. There were decorations in the trees; it was a beautiful sight indeed. Elder Arakawa and Haruto were pleased with how fast the clan had mobilized to get things ready. Aoi and Kenji had not been seen in the village, as they were preparing themselves for the wedding. The days went by fast and nobody had seen the bride or the groom until the morning of that day, when the sun was just rising over the mountains. In the training grounds, they stood together watching the sun rise. Haruto and Elder Arakawa had been watching from the temple steps; it was a day that the whole clan would remember.

The courtyard was filled with all the villagers dressed in their best attire; with gifts in hand for the wedding couple. Aoi and Kenji walked to the temple steps and greeted their parents and bowed. Arakawa told them that he had made some arrangements for a special guest to wed them. A Shaolin monk walked slowly out of the temple smiling at the couple and bowed; he was Aoi's Shaolin master from China. Aoi was surprised and could hardly contain herself, as she had tears of joy running down her face. Haruto held her arm and whispered in her ear to focus and channel her energy. Kenji stood next to Aoi and started to speak in a low voice so that only the very close could hear him; as he vowed to love her and be as one until time called upon him. Aoi did the same vowing her love to him and to keep the traditions of the Iga clan and teachings of the Shaolin within their family. The Shaolin monk gave them both sticks of smoking incense after he waved it over the couple and draped a black and golden sash over their wrists. They were now married, as they put the sticks in a vase in front of the statue of Buddha. As they walked into the courtyard, the village people cheered and threw flower petals that covered the ground as they walked.

As the wedding couple sat on the floor at the center of the long table with the parents on either side of them, the food started to come out. They were served first and then the parents and guests. There were some traditional dancers in the center of the room who showed the different katas of the Iga clan. They were slow and deliberate in their moves; it was a beautiful gift to the couple now married. Elder Arakawa gave them a Deed to a small property with a water buffalo and a pen full of geese. Haruto gave them a long wooden box; it held the Hanzo sword. The gifts were more than they could have asked for, and they were held in great honor and appreciation. After the dinner had been cleared away, Kenji and Aoi whispered to each other and nodded in agreement. They told all the guests that it would be their honor to show them their own dance and kata of love and appreciation. They stood up and wrapped the black and golden sash around their hands and arms and asked the Shaolin master to blind fold them as they walked to the center of the large room. Kenji was given the Hanzo sword by Haruto and Aoi had a new weapon to show the clan; a pair of short, broad knives with a unique style. They started their special kata and moved as one. Neither Haruto nor the Shaolin monk had seen this kata before. Aoi had put together the kata to add to the Black Dragon. It was one of the deadliest katas ever put together and it was meant to be used against heavily armored men on horseback or on foot. Haruto was amazed at the speed in which they moved, as he heard the swords singing in the air and the short, heavy knives flashing in the light. They moved as one. It was hard to see that there were two bodies moving within the kata; they had mastered the Dragon moves and added their own. When it was over, the clan was silent and all lowered their heads in respect knowing that they had all just witnessed an impossible feat of skill and precision. They were all honored that Keji and Aoi were part of the Iga clan, knowing that they would be there to protect them and fight to the death, if necessary.

The next few days were filled with anticipation. Kenji and Aoi would be getting the mark of the Black Dragon and they were now married. Elder Arakawa and Haruto both went to their new home and were ready to escort them to see the blacksmith. They saw that the village clan had been very generous with gifts of chickens and a couple of pigs. Kenji and Aoi greeted their parents and told them they were ready to take the mark. They all walked to the blacksmith's. The branding iron was buried in the red-hot coals. Haruto felt a second of hesitation as they entered the dark room, and asked them if they were ready to take the oath of the Black Dragon.

There were small beads of sweat forming on the foreheads of the couple. Aoi stated that she was willing to follow the teachings of the Black Dragon; to use the powers for justice, to help the poor, the weak, and victims of crimes. She would never use her teachings to enrich herself or her family. Aoi pulled her robe over her shoulders and turned her back to the blacksmith. He pressed the iron in between her shoulder blades, just below the neck. Aoi screamed, as she felt the heat go through her with a small hissing sound. Aoi held her ground and did not pass out. Haruto put the salve on the fresh burn. She felt as if ice had been placed on her back; it was very cool and smelled of green tea and other herbs. There was very little pain. Kenji stood in front of the coals and said that he would follow the teaching of the Black Dragon; to use the powers for justice against the criminals that plagued humanity. He vowed to find justice for his family no matter how long or how far his journey took him. The blacksmith took the iron out of the coals for a second time, as Kenji pulled his robe down and bared his chest. The red-hot iron was put on the left side of his chest above his heart. Kenji tried not to scream, but the intense heat was too much, as he yelled out feeling the heat enter his chest. Elder Arakawa held Kenji by the arm; he did not pass out. Haruto put the salve on his burn. The small white jar of salve was given to them and told them to put it on their burns for the next three days. Kenji and Aoi held hands as they walked back to their farm. They walked with confidence and pride and smiled at each other. Haruto looked at elder Arakawa and said, "This was a first; never before had there been two Black Dragons honored at the same time, and they have improved the fighting style. Aoi is a great warrior and teacher and she has just started a new life." Haruto replied, "Kenji has a new weapon of choice, the Hanzo sword. He will never be defeated when used for justice." Arakawa nodded in agreement.

That night, when Kenji and Aoi went to bed, Kenji laid on his back and Aoi laid on her stomach. They talked for hours about the feelings they had about their new roles with the clan and the responsibilities they would have for the rest of their lives. Kenji talked about the Hanzo sword and the power he felt when he held it. The sword was the sharpest weapon he had ever held and the balance and craftsmanship were unmatched. Aoi talked about how Japan was changing; the west had brought new weapons and technology and the cities were getting larger. Aoi was afraid that some of the old ways would be lost. She wanted to ensure that the knowledge of the clan was passed to the next generation.

The seasons passed with the years. Kenji and Aoi left the village several times over the years to do the work of the Black Dragon during the times of the Dragon Festival. The Yakuza now offered rewards, up to a million yen (Japan's currency) for the capture or death of The Black Dragon. The Black Dragon had been reported as being in several places at one time, which made the Black Dragon even a bigger mystery and legend.

Haruto knew it was time to tell Elder Arakawa that he was moving to a different region of Japan. The hard part was telling Aoi and Kenji. Japan was growing and so were the criminals. The City of Akita had seen enough bloodshed; the Yakuza had moved from the docks, as their numbers were greatly reduced, thanks to the Black Dragon. It was not wise for the Black Dragon to be in one area for a long time and now there were two others to think about. They must also find different areas to find the Yakuza.

It was early morning when Aoi met her father near the river fishing, and sat down next to him. He did not say anything as Aoi put her own line in the river. "I can't remember when we both were fishing at the same time," said Aoi. "I cannot remember a time either," replied Haruto. "Father, I have something to tell you." Aoi was looking down at her line in the water with tears in her eyes. "What is it that you would be so upset?" asked Haruto. "Father, Kenji and I must move from the village," replied Aoi. "We have been talking about it for weeks. Please do not ask us to change our minds; hear us out. There are too many of us in one location and Japan is growing. We are leaving for America. We are following our path. Many of our countrymen have left to work in the land called California. Kenji has seen the fliers asking for workers offering land and freedom," said Aoi. "The Black Dragon is known all over Japan and we are hunted every day. It would only be a matter of time before someone will betray us and call the soldiers asking for the reward." Haruto nodded his head and replied, "Everything you have said is true, but it is I, that is leaving, not you."

They spent hours at the river talking. In the end, it was settled; they both would be leaving the village. Kenji and Aoi would set off to the land of America and Haruto would find a new village or town to live in and hunt the Yakuza during the Festival of the Dragon. Haruto would have to find a new trade to peddle; maybe start a martial arts school. Aoi and Haruto got up from the river bank and started to walk away when Aoi said, "This is the first time that I have not caught any fish." Haruto smiled and said, "That is why we call it fishing instead of catching. We will have to pick someone to carry on with the training, as we will always be a part of the Iga clan and its traditions." Aoi nodded in agreement. Elder Arakawa was not upset. He talked of changes within Japan and the clan; it was time to move forward, and set a new path for the Iga clan.

Haruto pulled a small handcart behind him with everything he needed. The road to Kyoto was long and dangerous, if traveling alone. Aoi and Kenji were leaving from Akita by ship. That journey would also be very dangerous and long. The new adventures of the Black Dragon would continue in Japan and America.

In the months that followed, they all had reached their destinations safely; but not without being watched by everyone, and tested every step they took. Strangers were not welcome and, in America, Kenji and Aoi were told they could work on the railroads and in the mines. The women could stay within their own communities, doing laundry or cooking. Sometimes they were mistaken for Chinese and were called names, being treated like animals. The land was unforgiving and the food was hard to grow. They did not know the growing seasons of a new land. Kenji kept his chest wrapped and worked hard with the others that had traveled to the west. He learned to speak some of the English language and studied with Aoi at night, so they both could travel to better parts of California. They both saw the guns that most of the Americans wore on their belts and the horses they rode. They heard of the people that were driven away from their lands, called Indians; they were fierce warriors, like the samurai. Kenji and Aoi had much respect for them and their traditions.

Haruto was fortunate to find a small martial arts school with an old master looking for some help. His students were undisciplined and wanted things easy; they were the spoiled brats of the city's upper-class. After a small demonstration of his skills, Haruto was just the answer. The master did not test his skills, but did ask for some references. The name of Elder Arakawa got him to raise an eyebrow and a nod of respect. The time at the school would be good for him; he enjoyed training young minds and bodies of the spoiled upper-class.

7

A LAND OF MANY LAWS

IN A CITY called Santa Fe, in the southwestern United States, stood a small brick building of less than two thousand square feet. There were two restrooms, two small locker rooms with separate showers, and one small office. The rest of the area was dedicated to training areas. The walls had photos of her family lineage and weapons for training. Kana Arakawa stood alone in the center of the training floor and went through her kata of the Black Dragon. Kana closed her eyes and thought of all the training that had been passed down to her. She was young and beautiful; her feet barely touched the floor as she moved. She was graceful and fluid in her moves; moves that Aoi had passed on to her. Kana finished with a spinning jump into the air kicking her leg out; she had mastered the Dragon's Tail long ago. Upon landing on the floor, she had recovered in a low profile looking up. Kana had finished her early morning workout; it was time to get ready for her classes.

John Douglas had already finished his three-mile run and was getting ready to show up at Kana's Martial Arts Studio. He had gotten back from his studies in Japan six months ago and was very excited to see Kana again. He could not believe that he was able to get an opportunity of a lifetime to be her lead instructor at her new dojo. John remembered that he could write a book on just the new ways that he understood martial arts, after he studied with Kana; she was the real deal. John never pried into her business or asked about her personal interests. That would go against everything he had learned in Japan. His studio apartment was simple and clean. He had lost many girlfriends; due to his way of life, but he liked it; uncluttered and uncomplicated. His father, Fredrick Douglas, always kept tabs on him. He had invested thousands of dollars in his schooling and private flying lessons; after all, he was a Douglas. At nine o'clock, John walked into the dojo of his dreams and took off his shoes. He saw all the photos and weapons on the walls. His only question was how could someone so young, be so skillful in so many martial art forms. Kana must have been born doing a kata from the womb; her poor mother. He quickly snapped out of his day-dreaming to see Kana standing in the middle of the floor; he did not hear her walk in and that sort of spooked him.

Kana looked at John saying, "Welcome to your dojo; we will train and make warriors here. They will learn respect, honor, and justice." John slapped his hands to his sides and bowed from the waist. Kana asked if he was ready to show her that he had been keeping up with his training. John took his fight stance, smiled and said, "Always ready, Never surprised." Kana did a cartwheel to the wall that held wooden staffs, and kicked one in the air, in John's direction. Then she grabbed one, and vaulted herself six-feet from where he stood. John was amazed at how natural Kana made things look, but nothing could be further from the truth. Their training went on for twenty-minutes with John getting hit multiple times. He lost count after four; he was not able to touch her once; although he had tried. Training ended when Kana did a vault in the air and she tapped him on the top of his head; not hard, but just enough to let him know he would have a small bump on his head. John stood with his feet together, slapped his hands to his side and bowed, showing respect. Kana told him that a little ice would keep the swelling to a minimum and reminded him that he should not have been surprised. John smiled and would think about the next thing he would say and not be cocky about it.

At ten o'clock, several students showed up and took off their shoes as they entered; their ages varied from late teens to late fifties. Their training would have to be tailored to their physical abilities and John was happy to take the young ones. Kana was happy to teach the older ones, using the soft approach; how to use misdirection of strength against one's opponent. At one o'clock, another small group of students showed up; these were men and women in good physical shape.

They were off-duty police officers that wanted to keep up in their training and to learn new self-defense tactics. John had to shift gears; these people were here to learn and train. Kana told John that they would both be training this group. They would be advanced students who were allowed to come and go during any class, if they chose, to accommodate their work schedule. This policy helped boost her student numbers and the word had gotten out about her service to the community in doing so. It was four o'clock when the last student left for the day. John felt as if he had worked out all day. He had, and he was tired. It was time to call it a day, as he walked off the mat. John saw Kana on her knees in the corner of her office; as she held lighted incense over her head. He did not intrude, but walked quietly out the door.

Kana was sitting at her desk looking over her records and payments made to her business. She was happy to see that she had done well her first quarter. The decision to hire John was wise; he was young and strong with the desire to always learn and showed respect and honor. Kana remembered John from her last visit to Japan helping her grandfather train students from America. They paid high dollars to learn martial arts. Having a dojo in Japan was an honor and it came with many responsibilities to the people and the school. Training in Japan had no short cuts and it took years of training to become good at one's craft. John was a good student and did well in the art of Kyudo; which meant, The Way of the Bow; also known as Japanese archery.

Kana walked to her small apartment two blocks away. She lived in a condominium with another Japanese family next door. Hoshiko Watanabe was the grandmother who helped her daughter raise twin girls, Kiko and Michiko. Their mother, Aya, worked two jobs to support them. Aya's husband went missing, as he looked for work in San Francisco; that was three years ago. They never heard anything from the police after he was reported missing. They were too poor to hire a private investigator to investigate his disappearance. When Kana reached her door, Hoshiko greeted her with some flowers and said that a man in a dark car dropped them off. Kana did not know anyone that would do such a nice thing; could this have been John? She hoped that it was not; it would put a strain on their working relationship. She was not ready to be in a relationship as she had too much to do. When Kana got inside, she walked into the kitchen and got a vase for the flowers. When she unwrapped them, a small card fell on the counter. It read, "Ms. Arakawa, please accept these flowers as a token of my appreciation for your service to the community. Mr. Jefferson."

Kana did not remember the name nor did she have any students with that name; it was a mystery. She did not feel it was a threat of any kind but she would be more watchful in the future. In the days that followed, nothing was out of place. Students came and went and John was always early to work. Kana did not mention the flowers to John, but she did ask him if the name Mr. Jefferson meant anything to him. John replied that he did not know anyone by that name and went about his training. The following morning, as Kana walked to her dojo, she saw a black sedan parked in front of her building. Kana entered her dojo, took off her shoes and placed them to the side of the door. She saw two pairs of shoes; one belonging to John and the other was unknown;

but the person had very expensive tastes. She could tell by the style and quality of the leather. John was talking with a medium-build man with dark hair in the center of the room. John stopped talking and said, "This is Kana, the owner of this dojo." Kana walked up to the man and he placed his hands to his sides and bowed from the waist, introducing himself saying, "Ms. Kana, it is an honor to meet you. I hope you liked the flowers? My name is Mr. Jefferson." Kana looked at him and slowly bowed back and held out her hand to shake it, as it was the custom in America. "How my I help you, Mr. Jefferson?" replied Kana. "I hope we can help each other; may I have a few minutes of your time?" John took this as his cue to leave the room and so he walked into the locker room. "I'm not sure how to put this, so I will be direct, if you don't mind?" said Mr. Jefferson. Kana replied, "Please go ahead. I am not one to beat around the bush." "I represent a group of men sworn to protect this great nation from all enemies, foreign and domestic, since its birth. We are asking for your help to be one of many, to seek out justice where justice has been absent.

We are a country of many laws, but we have not been able to curb the criminal element by the laws we have instituted. Our politics and politicians no longer serve the people." Kana was not ready to jump at some stranger's offer to find criminals. She had her own agenda; an oath that she swore to keep and she had the seal of the Black Dragon on her back that would always remind her of her promise. Kana replied, "I need more time to think about this offer and I need more than just words. I want proof of this organization and I want to know more about you, sir." Kana was very direct with her words and it put Mr. Jefferson on the spot. "May I come back in a week to bring you all the information you seek?" asked Mr. Jefferson. "Sure, if that is all the time you need," said Kana. "Thank you for your time," said Mr. Jefferson, as he backed away and bowed as he left the building. Mr. Jefferson was on the phone as he pulled away saying, "She is everything we thought; she is going to be a tough cookie to crack, but worth it, if we can get her on board. I need all the information you can find on Ms. Arakawa and her entire family and I want all the information you can find on a John Douglas; his father is Fredrick Douglas, out of Vermont."

Kana turned to see John come out of the locker room. Kana asked John about Mr. Jefferson. John told her that he had just arrived a few minutes before she came in the door, and that he did not have to be told to take his shoes off before entering the mat area. He was well-dressed, so he thought that he was not here to work out. "Do you think he is the government type?" asked Kana. "I think he is more the private-sector type because he was too well dressed. What did he want?" replied John. "He was asking for my help, but I sense that there is a lot more to it than he's letting on," replied Kana. "I don't see him helping me; he said that we could help each other." John asked Kana, "What was with the flowers?" Kana said, "It wasn't personal; it was an acknowledgment. Are you ready to train?" "Yes," John replied, as he bowed and took two steps back. John thought about his last reply being cute, but ended up with a bump on the top of his head; he would not make the same mistake, and just show respect to his sensi. The training session went longer than normal. John was starting to feel his arms getting tired when Kana saw that he was starting to let his guard down. She stopped and told John to train on the climbing wall and rope three times a week to strengthen his arms and hands. The day's schedule was light and John was grateful. His arms and legs were sore from the days training. John looked at the small frame of Kana and did not understand how someone so small could be so strong and tireless. She was always focused. Kana always did things with purpose and with no wasted energy.

At the days end, John said his good-byes and Kana locked herself inside the dojo and went to her office. She had to make some inquiries about Mr. Jefferson. She did not trust easily, and he did not give her much information. It was time to call her grandfather and ask for guidance. Kana spent an hour on the phone speaking in her native language. It felt good to know that he was still master of tactics and deception. He was of the Iga clan, a Shinobi.

It was late that evening, when Kana arrived at home to see a small envelope stuck inside her door with a strange seal across it. Kana looked around and saw nobody in the area and tucked the envelope under her arm as she entered the kitchen area. She turned on the light; everything was in place and nothing had been disturbed. She put the envelope on the kitchen table and made a cup of tea, all the while looking at the envelope; as if it were going to get up and walk away. Kana sat at the table with her cup of tea. She looked at the seal; it was not made of wax or plastic, and the relief was that of the Lady of Justice holding the scales. Kana broke the seal and watched as it crumbled into a fine pile of silver dust. She had never seen anything like this before, and she put the dust into a napkin. A letter from the Justice Council read; "Ms. Kana Arakawa, we are a group of men and women that have been put in place since our great nation has been formed to ensure that our Constitution and The Bill of Rights are upheld. Unfortunately, our politicians and their politics have been turned upside down; they no longer serve the people or this great nation. Every faction of the criminal element have taken hold of all of our great cities that once thrived. Other countries are taking advantage of our good will and have raped our resources from under our noses. The politicians are making the people dependent on the government and the laws of this nation have been taking a back seat to the criminals. We are looking for Justice Seekers; those that want and believe in Justice for our families and this nation. We will use all of our resources from the past, and present, to bring to light the criminals that have strangled this country. We can offer you immunity from persecution, citizenship, training from our nation's finest, your home or business paid in full, food, lodging, transportation, all clothing, and equipment paid, and the gratitude of this great nation. Ms. Arakawa, this is a one-time offer and will last only three days. We hope that you will consider joining us; you would be an asset to the team.

This letter will self-destruct; the oils from your fingers have activated a chemical in the paper. Mr. Jefferson will contact you shortly. Sincerely, The Justice Council." No sooner had she finished reading, the letter was already falling apart and the ink had disappeared. Kana thought about the letter and its contents; there was no paper trail and no proof that she received a letter. All she had was a napkin of silver dust from the seal. She now had more questions than answers. Kana took out a note pad and started to write down questions for Mr. Jefferson. This Council did not pick her out of the air. They must have done some type of background check on her. What did they know about her? Kana was a model citizen. She had no criminal record, and all her bills were paid to date. They could not possibly know about the Black Dragon or her quest to find justice for her family. She was always very discreet when she traveled during the Festival of the Dragon. Kana found new places where the Yakuza and the Triad had control; mostly on the west coast in Asian communities.

Kana missed talking with her parents. Kenji died of pneumonia and had left her with a long wooden table that was disguised, and held the Hanzo sword. She used it as a tea table. Her mother, Aoi, was now living with a small group of elders. She was too old to take care of herself; but as a group, they did well. Kana remembered all the stories told to her, of the travels that Aoi had taken as a child, to America. Soon it would be time to visit her again; it would not be long before it was her time to pass. Kana was the last of her clan.

It was time to get some much-needed rest and think about her next move. Mr. Jefferson and the Justice Council were becoming more interesting by the day. It was four in the morning when Kana woke up from a premonition; it was as if her ancestors had told her to follow her path of justice; to train and pass on her knowledge of the clan. Then, she would find justice for her family. Kana's mind was clear; she knew what she had to do. Kana knew that her grandfather had come through for her once again. Kana was dressed and out the door at five

-thirty, and jogged to her dojo. It was an easy warm-up before she met John on the mat. Kana opened the door to her dojo at five-forty-five and took off her running shoes at the door. She went to the wall, which held several staffs, and decided to take a dark, hard wood staff that had some weight to it. Kana spun it around her body and above her head several times to get the feel of the staff. She went to the center of the mat and started her kata; the staff made a loud whirling sound as it moved faster than the other staffs on the wall, and did not flex. Kana sensed that someone was watching. As she was near the end of her kata, she stopped and stood at the ready, to face her observer. Mr. Jefferson was in the doorway and had taken his shoes off. He bowed as he faced Kana and apologized for interrupting her before she was done. Kana was upset and told him to enter at his own risk. Mr. Jefferson heard her tone and slowly walked to the center of the mat and knelt two feet from her and said, "Gomen nasai" (I'm sorry). Kana sat next to him with her staff beside her, and spoke to him as she looked into his eyes. "Answer my questions, without hesitation, and I will allow you to walk out of here without feeling my staff." A small bead of sweat appeared on his forehead and he agreed. Mr. Jefferson knew that he had to choose his words carefully and tell the truth. Kana felt as if she was being guided by her inner spirit and ancestors. Her questions would be to the point.

Kana asked, "Who are you, and what is your name?" Mr. Jefferson replied, "I go by Mr. Jefferson. My real name is of no consequence." Kana asked, "Why Mr. Jefferson? He replied, "I am a member of the Justice Council and we have taken the names of past U.S. presidents that had made a huge impact in our government. Our real names are of no consequence; only to those who wish us harm. This is why we are sworn to secrecy." Kana continued, "What is your job?"

Mr. Jefferson said, "I am a recruiter, facilitator, and investigator. I find the best of the best to become a Justice Seeker." Kana asked, "If I choose to become a Justice Seeker, how will you address me?" Mr.

Jefferson said, "You will be called #47 and I will be your handler; you will not take orders from anyone else." Kana asked, "Why #47?"

Mr. Jefferson explained that Justice Seekers are given the number of their state from which they were selected, at the time that state joined the union. "You will not know any of the names of other Justice Seekers; unless you have personal knowledge of said person; but at no time, will you use their name, only the number assigned to said person."

Kana asked, "Are the Justice Seekers working for the government?"

Mr. Jefferson said, "No, you would be a part of a secret group of people protecting the Constitution and the Bill of Rights from all enemies, foreign and domestic. You would bring justice to those that have used the system to escape justice and circumvent our laws through bribes, threats of life, and any other means to avoid the laws of this country." Kana asked, "Who would be the one that would determine who lives or dies?" Mr. Jefferson said, "The justice system, our law enforcement departments, and any evidence that the Justice Council has on record." Kana asked him how she would be able to help her mother monetarily or with any medical needs, as she does now? Mr. Jefferson answered, "All Justice Seekers are paid for their time as if employed by anyone; but, at a much higher rate than the average government worker. We would assist you with any arrangements that you wish to set up for your family." Kana asked, "What would happen in the event of my death defending this country's constitution from all enemies foreign or domestic?" Mr. Jefferson explained, "You would be treated with this country's highest honors and your family would never have to worry about anything." Kana asked, "Can I refuse a mission and walk away from this organization if I feel it is no longer a just cause?" Mr. Jefferson said, "You have no written contract, and if you feel that a mission is against your beliefs and it is wrong, state your feelings and sit it out. If you walk away, you will lose all benefits and pay. You will be on your own, never to be contacted again." Kana asked why she was chosen. Mr. Jefferson said, "Ms. Arakawa, you are the best of the best. Your lineage goes back over two-hundred years and you and your family have been trained by Shaolin monks; you are of the Iga clan, known as ninja or Shinobi. I know that you are all about family, honor and justice."

Kana told Mr. Jefferson, "So, you have done your homework. I will give you my answer over tea tomorrow at four o'clock; after I have taught my last class for the day." Mr. Jefferson thanked Kana saying, "Ms. Arakawa, no matter what your answer is, you have my respect. It has truly been my pleasure to meet and talk with you." Mr. Jefferson got up from his knees and walked out of the dojo, as he said hello to John has he passed by him. John looked at him and saw that Mr. Jefferson was deep in thought as he walked to his car. Kana stood in the center of the mat and waited for John.

John asked Kana if everything was alright? Kana looked at John and smiled, as she spun her staff around her body and said, "Always ready Never surprised." John went to the wall and picked out a staff that he was accustomed to, and spun it around his body before coming at attention and bowing his head saying, "Ready, sensi." John was on his game, but the sound of Kana's staff made him more defensive in his moves. He was not sure why, but it helped him from getting hit.

Kana was pleased with John's training; he was learning fast and he was confident. Kana saw that he listened to his surroundings and made defensive moves without really understanding why; he was becoming more aware of danger.

The day was normal with all the students; that is, until closing time when five hard-looking Asians came in the door and stepped on the mat without taking their shoes off. John approached them and asked them to take their shoes off, and to show some respect. One of the men showed his handgun in his waistband and told him not to be a hero. John stopped in his tracks and asked, "What do you want?"

The man asked, "Are you the owner?" John said, "No, she is over there near the wall." The other men walked toward John and pulled out their guns. "There is no need for violence; please put your guns away. We are peaceful here," said Kana. Their leader walked on the mat towards Kana and said, "Welcome to the neighborhood. You have not paid your protection tax yet, and you are overdue." "How much would that be, to keep all the trouble away?" asked Kana. "That would be twelve hundred for the month and another for last month," replied the man. "What if I don't have that kind of money every month?" asked Kana. The man laughed and said, "I think you will have to bury one of your students every week until you pay, or sign your property over to us." Kana asked, "Is there no other way?" "Not unless you want to work it off, say three nights a week?" The other men started to laugh and waved their guns. John sat on the mat and watched as Kana slowly moved to the center of the mat while she talked to the men. The men surrounded her and looked at her like fresh meat to a pride of lions. Kana said, "Then, so be it; I will dance in your blood and stand on your bones before I or any of my students die." Kana slowly started her kata, as she moved in small circles, as the men watched and laughed, saying she is going to be fun. The man who held his gun on Kana looked on, as the gun was kicked out of his hand. It happened so fast that he did not know what to do, as a knife blade went into his heart; he only felt a soft breeze across his face, as he fell to the floor. The other men looked down at their leader; it was the last thing they saw, as each one fell to the mat with a look of surprise on their faces. The wounds to each body were the same; one stab wound to the heart.

John had watched the whole event unfold in front of him. He was in shock and in awe at the speed of Kana and her moves. He had never seen or heard of anything like what had happened in front of him. John did not know what to do next, as he got up and walked towards Kana. Kana asked him if he had been hurt and John just shook his head no, as he looked at the bodies on the mat. Kana was cool and calm as she talked softly to John, as she walked him to her office and made him some tea. Kana called the only person she knew that could help, Mr. Jefferson. It was not fifteen minutes before a group of men came through the doors with plastic booties and gloves and carrying a large roll of plastic. Mr. Jefferson followed behind them, with plastic booties on as he walked across the mat towards John and Kana. Mr. Jefferson asked John if he could talk about what he had seen. John looked at Kana before asking, "Do I need a lawyer?" Kana told John to just tell the truth. Mr. Jefferson heard John talk for thirty minutes until he started to repeat himself; then stopped him. Kana looked at Mr. Jefferson saying, "Yes, is my answer now, on one condition; I get to follow up on any leads where those men came from. There will be more coming when they don't return." Mr. Jefferson looked into Kana's eyes and said, "You will find out with or without my help; it is who you are. Welcome to the fold #47, and thank you." Kana could see that this had been the first time that John had ever been threatened with death and it was the first time that he had ever seen Kana's true abilities. John would be fine in a day or two; seeing death, first hand, is always a shock to the system the first time. Mr. Jefferson asked if he could take John home and Kana thought that it was a good idea. She knew that John would have to be debriefed on the events that had occurred; no police were called to the scene, and the cleanup was as if nothing had ever happened on the mat; even their cars were towed away. Kana had some homework to do on her Asian assailants. They had to report to somebody, and she wanted to know who the big fish in the pond were, so she could pay them a visit. That night, a courier dropped off an envelope to Kana, with the five names, gang affiliations, and their last known addresses. Mr. Jefferson beat her to the punch and had done her homework for her; plus, he had a small, average-looking sedan dropped off for her to use, while on assignment. She could see that she had made the right choice with Mr. Jefferson. Kana was surprised that all correspondence did not last long, as it started to disintegrate after she touched the paper. How clever, she thought; no trace of messages. Kana had to memorize everything she read from Mr. Jefferson.

Kana had been on the road for one day and had everything she needed for the hunt. She realized that she did not have to go very far to find criminals in her area, thanks to Mr. Jefferson. Kana could not figure out why there were so many Asians in the surrounding area; so, she went to the local college library. Kana found out that Amache, Colorado had been a former Japanese internment site. Many displaced Japanese had found their way to Arizona and surrounding states; therefore, the criminals followed the weak. They were used to praying on them, by using their own culture against them. The Japanese were a very private people and they took care of their own business. Kana thought it was time to remind them of the Black Dragon from their own country.

8

MAKING IT OFFICIAL

KANA SAT IN her car, parked in the front parking lot of a laundry mat, and watched as young men went upstairs to an apartment. The foot traffic could not be missed if anyone bothered to watch; her last count was at fifty-seven people in six hours. Kana did not see any bags or drugs. She thought about the possibilities of what items could be so lucrative; information, gambling markers, and credit cards. She needed more information, so she thought of a night operation.

The night was warm, with only a slight breeze coming from the South. Kana was dressed completely in black with soft, black rubber shoes made for climbers. Her only weapons were two knives in her sleeves and several throwing stars; she did not want to make any contact tonight, but one always had to be ready for anything. Kana slipped into the dark of night, unseen, as she worked her way to the rear of the building. She scaled the wall, using the windows and gutters to make her way up to a small window of the apartment that had lights on. People were still showing up. Kana hung upside-down and looked into the apartment; there were several people in line at a table, and a woman was on a computer putting in numbers from each person that stood in front of her. The woman took cell phones and exchanged them for another one. She handed an envelope to the man, as the next person stood in line. Kana could not figure out what was being exchanged, so she thought that she would take the next person who left the building and ask him nicely about his exchange. Kana was running around the building when she nearly ran into a man that was walking around the building, smoking a cigarette. Kana stood against the wall of the building near a rain gutter; the man walked right passed her and did not even see her. Kana followed the man into the dark; as her victim was unaware of her presence, only two feet away. There was a buzzing sound and the man reached into his pocket, took out a cell phone and read the text. He tapped in his reply and put his phone away. Kana hit the man with her hand in a classic blade-hand strike at the base of the man's head. The man fell like a sack of potatoes; he was out cold. Kana went through his pockets and took his phone and wallet and saw that he had tattoos on his neck. He had a semi- automatic handgun and a large knife in his waistband; she took it all, including his shoes. Nobody would guess who his assailant was; leaving the man with nothing, was just misdirection; something that she had learned long ago. Kana was about to leave the area for the night, but opportunity showed itself again, as another man pulled up in a car next to hers and was getting ready to walk towards the apartment. Kana struck again, from the dark, and hit the man across his throat; then behind his head with her blade-hand. The man fell hard between the cars. Kana searched him and took everything he had, even his watch and necklace. Kana got into her car and drove away unseen.

Kana needed help to extract all the information from the phones and get a better understanding of what was being traded. All she knew, was that it was organized crime, but not the Yakuza, as she had first thought. Kana knew who she could ask, but how to contact him was another question. The drive home was without incident and very boring. She rather enjoyed getting out and testing her skills. Kana was tired and ready to go to bed when she arrived home. But as she pulled up to her condo, she saw two black SUVs parked in the front. She slowly passed by them, unable to see inside the vehicles. She made the decision to park and be ready for anything. It was Mr. Jefferson; the first thing he did was smile, saying, "Yes, I had a tracker on your car. I was just keeping tabs on one of my best recruits. We still have a few things to finish up." Once Kana got closer, several men were standing by and offered to take the phones and other items that she had recovered from her trip. Kana gave all the items to the men and looked at Mr. Jefferson, "So what do we have to finish?" asked Kana. "May we step inside? I have something for you," replied Mr. Jefferson. They stepped inside the door and Mr. Jefferson gave her a small box. "I will need you to repeat after me." She repeated, *"I, Kana Arakawa, do solemnly swear to keep all secrets and knowledge of the Justice Council and Justice Seekers to myself. I will uphold and defend the Constitution of the United States and the Bill of Rights from all enemies, foreign or domestic, and keep safe all citizens from said enemies at all costs; to bring justice and hope to all law-abiding people without prejudice. From this day forward, I will be known as # 47 to the Justice Seekers and assist the team, in any way possible, to complete the mission. I may be released from my oath upon my death or permission from the Justice Council with just cause."*

Kana opened the small box and saw a silver Lady Justice pin, holding the scales. She now believed that she was a part of something bigger than herself; she was a part of a team. Mr. Jefferson told her to wear the pin on her collar when on mission, so that other Justice Seekers could identify her as someone they could trust with their lives. Mr. Jefferson then turned and introduced her to Mr. Lincoln. He smiled and shook her hand saying, "Young lady, make us proud and do what you do best." Then he bowed. Kana felt honored and bowed back saying, "I will follow my path of justice, as my family has taught me." Mr. Jefferson told #47 that he would get back with her to explain the protocols of the Justice Seekers and to give her all the information that she had gathered from her mission. The men left as she stood in the living room with the small box, still in her hands. Kana was wiped out; and, at the same time, her head was swimming with tons of information she was trying to process. She went into the kitchen and made some tea to calm herself down, so she could get some much-needed sleep.

It was late morning when Kana woke to the knocking at her door. It was John. The dojo was still locked and he was afraid that something had happened to her; he had waited two hours before running to her condo to check on her. Kana let him inside and asked him if he would have tea with her. He respectfully turned her down and asked if he could have some water instead. Kana nodded her head and gave him a bottle of water. John kept his eyes down; he did not want to look her in the eyes. She noticed, and asked, "John, what is going on with you? You can always talk to me." John looked at her and said, "Mr. Jefferson made me an offer and it would require me to leave and go back east." Kana smiled and said, "I see, and you only have three days to except his offer, right?" John was about to say something, but Kana cut him off and told him not to worry, and that she was sure that there would be a day in the future when they would meet again. John smiled and said, "I know we will; Always ready, Never surprised." "When do you leave?" asked Kana. John looked down and said, "Tonight." Kana looked at him and told him to train hard and never look back; you have a bright future ahead of you. John smiled and bowed saying, "Sensi, it has been my honor to train with you. I will never forget you." Kana bowed back, saying that the honor was hers. Kana could see that John had tears in his eyes, as he left and thought he would be #14, if her memory served her right.

Kana walked to the dojo and opened the doors; it was clean and the mats looked brand new. She took off her shoes and walked across the mats to the wall with all the staffs and weapons and started to take them down. Kana had to give notice to all her students that she would have to close until further notice; it made her sad but, it was for the greater good. The students that came into the dojo were saddened at the new and wanted to help, but she saw no way to keep her doors open. The last group of students arrived at the dojo; they were the off-duty police officers that were there to brush up on their skills. Kana met them and told them the bad news and the Patrol Sergeant smiled and said, "I have some very good news for all parties concerned". He handed her a white envelope with the department's letterhead, that said that the police department has received a grant for two-million dollars to rent and renovate Kana's building until she returns; at which time, she will take over all responsibilities for said building and training of all police officers. Kana thought about the timing, and knew that Mr. Jefferson had a hand in the grant. Kana was now free to spend full-time with the Justice Seekers; but, she was not finished yet;. She still had to find out who was the head of the snake.

The last session with the police officers was more of a walk-through of the building; taking down old photos and weapons from the walls and boxing them up until she was able to return. Kana finished up and handed the keys to the Patrol Sergeant and told him to take good care of the place. Kana walked home a little sad that she no longer had a place to call her own; her condo was not a training area and she was going to miss that.

There was a knock at the door and a woman dressed in blue slacks and a white blouse stood at her door. She had a lady justice pin on her collar. Kana smiled and opened the door and offered her to step inside. The woman smiled and thanked her as she walked inside. She introduced herself. "I am #43. I have been assigned to help you get up to speed on our protocols when on mission and answer all of your questions for the next two weeks. We are going to be a team; I am to follow you and help you finish your business with those who wished you harm." Kana bowed her head and said, "I am #47. I mean no disrespect, but I do not need a partner." "Nor do I," said #43, "but you are my responsibility for two weeks and I am not going to fail Mr. Jefferson". Kana smiled and said, "Very well, I have a small couch or you can sleep on the floor. You are welcome to the kitchen and food." That night, #43 sat with #47 talking about communications, firearms, clean up and team work with the Justice Seekers. It was late, and Kana wanted to get some rest before asking about finishing her mission with #43. #43 had some peppermint tea and fell asleep on the couch. Kana went to bed thinking about how the next few weeks were going to work out with #43; she was nice and very informative, but could she take care of herself?

Kana woke up early to get some tea, only to find that the tea pot was hot and the tea was waiting for her on the kitchen table. #43 had made some tea and was sitting with her legs crossed and her eyes closed. She was meditating; waiting for #47 to awaken. Kana sat at the table sipping her tea and felt a slight breeze across her face. #43 was sitting at the table with a cup of tea facing #47. #47 smiled and said, "I see you have some training; may I ask who you studied under?" #43 replied, "I studied under Master Katsumi in Japan for ten years. My father was in the Air Force, so we moved around a lot; he enrolled me in the school to get me to focus more on my studies. It worked. I really took to martial arts and stuck with it. This was until my father told me that he wanted me to work in the private sector, which meant that I had to leave for the mainland to continue my studies. The rest is history, and here I am with you now." Kana did not know if it was a coincidence that she had trained under her grandfather. Mr. Jefferson had done his homework on her history. #43 was going to be a good fit for two weeks, but she still wanted to test her skills.

After morning tea, #43 asked if #47 was ready to travel; she had information on the Asian's gang; the phones led to a web of gangs up and down the I-25 corridor into Colorado. Their first stop would be in a city called Pueblo, Colorado; this was an area of known organized crime that included human trafficking and cattle rustling. The head of the snake, that #47 was looking for, was pulling all the strings for hundreds of miles in every direction.

During the drive into Colorado, #43 asked #47 what her plan was, once they got into the area. #43 stated that they needed to do a soft recon of the office area where the phones were being downloaded. #47 told #43 that they would walk right into the office and ask for a job, saying that they were replying to a Help Wanted ad in the paper. #43 smiled and said, "Walking right into the hornets' nest and stirring the pot; that should get you some results." #47 looked at #43 and said, "Having second thoughts about being my partner?" #43 laughed and said, "Not in this lifetime."

Kim Hung Lo was young, ambitious, and smart. He came from a long-established crime family out of China. His cousin and his friends were missing. The only information he had was that his cousin had gone out to shake down new businesses to enlarge their territory. They didn't like walking around stealing information from phones; there was no excitement in that. The downloading of information from the phones had been used by China to gain access into personal banking, and in some cases, the photos captured were good for blackmail. Kim didn't like being tucked away in a strip mall, but his superiors didn't want to draw any attention from law enforcement. His job was simple; download the phones, send the encrypted information to China, and stay under the radar. Kim had to figure out a way to find his cousin without his uncle knowing he was missing. Kim made a call to one of his most trusted enforcers, Lee Chang, and asked him to find his cousin and bring him home before his father got involved; his father had the worst temper.

Lee Chang did not like cleaning up messes and he was no babysitter. He took pride knowing that he was a good assassin and hunter of men. His preferred weapon of choice was a pair of knives that were custom made for him. He was more of a traditionalist and wanted to make killing personal by looking into the eyes of his victims, as life left the body. He refused to use guns; they were loud, could be traced, and it took very little skill to shoot. Now he was tasked with finding Kim's cousin and his crew. If they were in a jail cell somewhere, it would mean a death sentence for them when they got out. The powerful heads of the families would not tolerate such carelessness and did not like being a conversation piece in the news.

The road trip to Colorado was almost over, as they crossed state lines. It would be at least another two-and-a-half hours to Pueblo. #43 looked over at #47 and asked, "Are you really just going to walk in the building and ask for a job?" #47 laughed and said, "You have been holding that in for hours, and now you want to know my plan?" "It sounded a little crazy to me, but maybe you are on the right path to a quick death. I have some questions before we go busting up their party," replied #43. #47 pulled over into a gas station and parked the car. "OK, we are going to make a plan now, before we get there. Will that make you happy?" #43 looked at #47 and said, "We never put a Justice Seeker in harm's way without having a plan." #47 realized that she was right; she had to be responsible as she was no longer working alone. #47 apologized and told her that she was focused on the mission. #43 told her to remember that part of the mission was to gather all information possible for the Justice Council and to remember the big picture. #43 was right. #47 was learning what it was to be a Justice Seeker. "Now, if you have been good, I have a present for you. I have been dying to give it to you since being assigned as your partner." #43 went to the trunk of the car and pulled out a black bag; a wooden box was inside the bag. #47 saw the box and she knew it was from Japan, by the way it was made. "Go ahead and open it; it is from Japan," said #43. #47 took the box and opened it. There were a pair of knives and several throwing stars and darts with a small white porcelain jar. It was from her grandfather.

#47 looked at #43 and asked, "How much do you know about me?" #43 said, "Before I was assigned this mission to be your partner, I studied under your grandfather without knowing about you. Mr. Jefferson had asked if I would take the mission to protect you. I was only able to put two and two together after seeing some of your pictures hanging in your house. I know that you do not need protecting; your skills are far beyond mine, but we have been trained in the same philosophy and style." #47 smiled and said, "Yes, we have something in common and I will do my best to show you the ways of my clan to continue in your training, if you so desire." "I would be honored to be your student, thank you," replied #43. Within an hour, they had formulated a plan. Once they got into Pueblo, they would put their plan into action and see what they could find out. #43 showed #47 her own weapons that she had in the trunk. There were three knives and several darts; two of the knives went into her boots and the other, behind her neck, hidden by her hair. The darts went into the waist band of her pants. Now she was ready to help stir up the hornet's nest.

9

DIFFERENT COUNTRY
SAME SNAKE

KIM HUNG LO was looking around his office and saw nothing out
of place. Other offices had as many as ten people in line to pick up or
drop off phones. Kim thought that it was funny to see that the Americans did not pay attention to what they bought or asked any questions
about the product's functions. Americans always wanted the newest
electronic items that hit the market; TV's, stereos, cameras, refrigera-
tors, and computers. All of these items had been modified in some way
to spy and steal information from the consumer without their knowledge. They were even buying weapons made in China; guns, knives,
and ammunition, were all cheaply made and inferior. The information
that he got from the phones would generate billions of dollars for the
crime families and he was an important cog in the wheel. The situation
with his cousin was on his mind. But it was more about the fallout he
would receive if something bad had happened; he would be blamed.

Sending Lee to find his cousin was overkill with the use of an assassin, but he could be trusted and he could find anyone.

The building was in the downtown area with street parking. There were people walking in and out most of the buildings. #47 saw a stack of fliers next to a store, took several, and turned to the Help Wanted ads. #47 saw what she was looking for; the office building next to the one they were walking into, was asking for day help. #47 circled it in red pen and looked at #43 saying, "We have our ticket inside." #43 looked at #47 and said, "I hope we find the snake". "So do I," replied #47.

#47 and #43 walked up the stairs and opened the door to suite B. A man met them at the door immediately, and asked how he could help them. #47 held up the paper ad to his face saying. "I am not leaving until I get an interview. I want to see the office manager." The man replied, "You have the wrong office. We don't need any help." #43 looked around and said, "How can you say you don't need the help; look at all these people standing around." They were making enough noise to get Kim's attention from his office, as he walked out to meet them. #47 and #43 both saw a gun in his waistband and they immediately went to plan B. The big man that was trying to hold them back, grabbed his neck and fell to the floor. #47 had put a dart in his neck; he would not bother them anymore. Kim did not see why his man fell to the floor, but he reached into his waistband to grab his gun. The two women stood looking at the big man holding his hands over his mouth, as if in shock. Kim was an arm's length of #47 and was trying to put his gun away, thinking they were not a threat. That was a huge mistake on his part, as #43 kicked him between the legs contacting his "family jewels." Kim turned white in the face and wanted to vomit, as he doubled over in pain that he had never felt before. #47 looked around and saw people standing around looking at Mr. Lo on the floor; they were not soldiers, just mules of information. #47 ordered all of them to put their phones into the wastebasket and step back to the wall. They did as they were ordered; all but one, who wanted to challenge them as he stepped towards them. #47 asked him if he was ready to die? The man smiled and said that we all must go sometime, it may as well be now, as he took out a knife from the small of his back. #43 stepped in front of #47 saying, "This one is mine," as she took two knives from behind her back. The man said, "Alright, now we have a real fight; ladies first?" #43 didn't take the bait and stood her ground waiting to see what kind of training the man had up his sleeve to feel so confident. The man lunged at her, went into a fight stance, and changed the position of his knife in his hands. #43 saw that he was trained, but nowhere near her level of training; maybe he was bluffing, so she let him try again. The man went into a boxing mode with his knife; trying to cut her as he struck at her. #43 cut his arm as he reached out with the knife. He pulled his arm back and looked at the cut. The man tried again; this time he tried to cut her face. #43 cut him across his stomach and cut off part of his ear in retaliation. The man cursed her and lost control of his temper; he was now swinging his knife wildly from side to side, hoping to make contact. #43 watched and took her time in picking her target. #43 cut the wrist holding the knife; the knife hit the floor as the man looked up at #43. He watched as she spun in small circles, making several cuts to his face and body. When #43 stopped, the man was barely standing in a pool of his own blood. He fell to his knees as #43 made the final cut; the man's head hit the floor before his body, and there were screams from the on-lookers as they reeled in shock at the sight of the dead man. Kim had seen the death of one of his men and he knew he was no match for them. He could barely stand up and felt very weak, but he was willing to give them anything they wanted at this point. #47 dragged Kim over to his desk and put him in his chair. #47 checked the drawers for any weapons and took away his semi-auto. She took it apart, throwing parts of it out of the window. #47 asked him if he was the person in charge of the gang that threatened her life and that of her students. Kim said that the man in question was his cousin, but was working on his own; his father was a member of one of the largest crime families out of China. He explained that he oversaw the gathering of information to send to China. #43 asked, "What type of information?" Kim said, "All kinds of information; anything they can get from your phones, mostly." #43 asked, "How much money are you talking about?" Kim said, "Billions, every year." #43 asked #47, "Are we done here? #47 replied, "Yes," as she broke Kim's neck with a twist. This snake was dead, but there were many others. All she had to do was be patient. Working with the Justice Council as a Justice Seeker was interesting and challenging. #47 thought that #43 was excellent in her fighting skills and had the right temperament using good judgment.

#43 and #47 walked out of the office building with a trash bag full of phones and laptop computers. The people there had run out of the building afraid that they might be next on the chopping block. "I don't think that the police will find anyone to question. What do you think?" asked #43. "I think my mission is over and I can get back to training, being a Justice Seeker," replied #47. "Agreed; from this day forward, there will be no witnesses and we will be leaving calling cards with our targets," said #43. #47 asked, "What was the calling card?" #43 took out a small card, the same size as a business card, only it was all white with a "Justice Served" printed in the middle of the card. She explained, "We place these cards with our targets, so the police and criminals know it was not a random killing. The people that become targets are the ones that have gotten away from law enforcement and have used unlawful means to escape prison; like drug lords, sex traffickers, and people using dirty cops and public officials. We will avoid all cameras, ATM's, traffic cameras, and anything that could capture our image and get us recognized by any law enforcement agency in the world. Remember, the bad guys have tech and have people working for them also." #47 was amazed at how many protocols she had to remember to keep every-one safe. She was very grateful to have #43 explain everything while they were together. #47 had a question for #43 and asked, "When do we unload all of this trash to Mr. Jefferson? And how soon can we get back, so I can close up my house?" #43 smiled saying, "It sounds as if you like the idea of becoming a Justice Seeker." #47 replied, "It beats any other offer I've gotten lately; and by the way, your skills with a knife are exceptional." #43 said, "Thank you. That means a lot coming from you. I know your skills are far superior to mine."

#43 started the car and headed South on I-25 and said, "It's time to go home and unload this information." #47 told #43 to pick a spot to eat within the next hundred miles. In the meantime, she was going to catch a nap, if it was OK. #43 told her that she hoped that she liked Mexican food. #47 said she could eat anything at this time. #43 said, "I'll wake you when we get to a good spot to eat; so no worries." #43 turned on the radio and found a classic rock station that was playing some good driving music; "Born to be Wild" by Steppenwolf never sounded so true.

Three hours later, #43 woke #47 from a deep sleep, who was curled up in the back seat. #43 was saying, "Wake up, sleepy head, we are here. #47 looked up and saw the sign, "The Wok". #43 smiled at her and told her that she thought that she would surprise her and let her sleep. I had some good driving music to help me stay awake. #47 said it was a good surprise; sat up and said, "Let us eat; I am hungry." They both walked inside and waited until their eyes adjusted to the lack of light. They scanned the room, as they were shown to their table; it was not busy. They both ordered tea and looked at the menu. It was the normal menu; nothing special. #47 ordered Combination Lo Mein, Peking Duck, stir fried vegetables with egg rolls and wonton soup. #43 looked at her and asked," You hungry?" "Starving," replied #47. #43 ordered Sesame Chicken with white rice, egg rolls with sweet and sour sauce. The waitress was attentive and kept asking if they needed anything. Both #43 and #47 smiled and thanked her. During the meal, #47 scanned the room and watched the door. #43 told her to slow down and chew; #47 did not realize that she was eating fast. She slowed down, and said that wanted to get back as soon as possible; she had a bad feeling that something was wrong. "In that case, let's get out of here," replied #43. The waitress smiled and said thank you, as they left the table. They did not want to wait for the bill so they left two, one-hundred-dollar bills on the table. As they got into the car, #47 said that her mother always told her to listen to her feelings, and never ignore her stomach. #43 laughed and said, "Well your stomach must have told you that it's your inner feelings talking, because you sure ate enough food to keep your stomach busy for a few days." #43 put her foot on the gas, as she pulled away and left some tire marks on the road. It was not long before they pulled up to her condo, and #47 told her to keep driving to her dojo, just down the road. As they got closer to her dojo, #43 and #47 could see several police cars with their lights on, that blocked the entrance. They pulled off to the side of the road and watched as police officers, with their guns out, pointed them at the door. #47 got out and ran behind one of the police cars and yelled at the officer that she was the owner of the dojo and wanted to know what was going on. The officer told her that they had received a 911 call from one of their own, that was inside the building; that a man was inside threatening four officers at knife point, before he was cut off. There were no shots fired or demands made; it was just quiet. Just then, several shots were fired with a scream from an officer. #47 watched as the door opened just enough for a head to come rolling out. It was that of the police officer who had gone inside. The police officer that had been watching the door was in shock, as he reported it to dispatch and asked for backup; code 3, officer down, shots fired.

#43 and #47 where next to the officer, and told him that the police should not enter the building until they knew the threat. #47 looked at #43 and told her to keep the officer safe and not allow any more police to enter the building until she was able to contact them; she was going into the building. The officer asked them who they are, and the reply was, "We are here to keep you safe; this is our job." #47 looked at #43 and told her that this was her responsibility; her fight, as she ran to the side of the building and disappeared. Moments later, she waved her hand to the police officer from the top of the building. The officer asked #43, "How did she do that?" #43 replied, "If I told you, I'd have to kill you; just kidding. I've always wanted to say that."

#47 saw the small window above her office and climbed inside. She hit the floor without a sound. #47 opened a small box from under her desk and took out a change of clothes. #47 was dressed in the classic ninja black with extra throwing stars, darts and a short sword. She scanned the dojo and saw the dead bodies on the floor; five plain-clothed officers in gym attire and one headless body of the police officer near the door. #47 could sense a presence inside, but could not see the killer. There was a change in the air; the smell of blood was starting to fill the gym. #47 looked up to see that there was a man dressed in black, looking down into the gym. He was not dressed as a ninja; it was more like a body suit. #47 knew that he was an assassin and well trained; but who was he, and what was his mission? She had many questions, but she had no time to ask them. She heard sirens in the distance. The assassin was running out of time; he had to try to escape. #47 used an old trick from her grandfather and whispered, "I see you; I am the Black Dragon and I will dance in your blood and stand on your bones before I die." That did the trick. The man moved from the rafters to the floor and looked around. He broke his silence and said, "I have heard about you; I thought you were just a myth from the old country. Show yourself." The man took out his knives and held them in the ready fighting stance. The man slowly turned and looked in every direction. He was getting his nerve up, and knew that he was running out of time; he had to push his agenda. "Where are the men that came here?" asked the assassin. "Who are you?" came the reply. "I am Lee Chang; my boss has entrusted me with their return." "Why did you kill innocent police officers?" asked #47. "They were collateral damage," replied Chang. "As was your boss, Kim Hung Lo," replied #47. The man was livid and asked for the Black Dragon to show himself. "I am here," as she cut him across his right Achilles tendon. The man went down to one knee and swung his arm, cutting the air, but made no contact. #47 stood in front of Chang so he could see her; she was out of harm's way when he jumped up on one leg, swung his arm and tried to cut her. #47 cut his arm for his efforts, as he tried again; and again, #47 cut his bicep and his artery. Chang swung his other arm and tried to limp away, but was met seeing the Black Dragon in front of him. #47 cut him again, across his forehead and blinded him with his own blood. Chang was swinging wildly, realizing that he was dying. "Are you Triad?" asked #47 "Yes, I work for Jiao-Ling in China." "You failed your mission; kill yourself, or I will do it for you," replied #47. Chang put his knife to his chest and hesitated for a fraction of a second, before the Black Dragon hit the handle of the knife with her open hand and drove the knife to the pummel into his chest. Chang was dead and she would remember the name Jiao-Ling.

#47 heard the police loud speaker from the police car order the occupants of the building to exit. She ran to her office and gathered her clothes; went back through the roof, where she changed her clothes, and ran around the building to call #43. The police were going to enter the building, and she did not want to be in the area. #43 saw #47 wave her hand and point to the car. #43 got the message and ran to the car. As they both got into the car, the police made their way into the dojo. #43 slowly pulled away, not wanting to draw attention; there would be too many questions. This incident would be national news within minutes.

The news station announced that six police officers were killed by a Chinese gang member who had ambushed five, unarmed off-duty police officers; He had killed them at a gym, and killed one on-duty officer who had responded to the scene. The Chinese gang member killed himself when confronted by several police and SWAT, as they entered the gym. That was the story the news was pushing; it said nothing about the police officer who had contacted the owner of the gym or that he was unable to verify and identify the owner. This got the officer suspended, without pay, for two weeks, and was reassigned to a desk.

10

REAL COWBOYS

#47 AND #43 had several more days to work together, and #47 was thinking on her feet, keeping most of the protocols in place. All the phones and information from the laptop computers had been delivered to Mr. Jefferson. Both were given an assignment in Colorado, as thanks for all their hard work. There was a knock at #47's door; it was a courier with two large black duffel bags and keys to a dark blue GMC Yukon. #47 looked at #43 and they smiled as they looked at the courier's collar. He had a Lady Justice pin showing; as he left, he smiled and said, "Happy hunting". #43 reminded #47 to make sure she was careful when handling any documents, as they all were treated to disintegrate after touching them. #47 looked around as she closed the door. They felt like kids in a candy shop when they opened the bags. There were ear wigs, two small radios, clothing, boots, Bench made pocket knives, a 35mm digital Cannon camera with a telescoping lens, top grade night-vision glasses, two M&P 380 Shield EZ with suppressors, two hundred rounds of JHP, plus one-hundred-thousand dollars in cash, and a box of Justice Served cards. #47 told #43 that she really had no use for guns; she knew how they worked, but never had any training with guns. #43 told her not to worry; "The training will come soon. We must know about all types of guns and, at least, know how to use the basic guns used by our enemies." #47 agreed and said that she would learn more about them and carry one if the mission called for it and for the safety of others. #43 reminded her of an old saying, "Never bring a knife to a gun fight," that is, unless you are #47. She laughed knowing that she could handle herself very well, without a gun. They checked out their "wheels"; the GMC Yukon was big, and it could hold everything they had to pack and then some. "So why do you think Mr. Jefferson gave us such a big vehicle?" asked #47. "I'm not sure, but it should blend in with our mission," replied #43.

There was also a large folder with maps and information about their contacts. Apparently, there were two ranchers that had witnessed some cattle rustling and there were several dozen females that were put into a smaller refrigeration truck; they were all handcuffed together. There was also a dozen armed men. The men followed the trucks at a distance. They called the State Police, but they never showed up. #43 asked if cattle rustling was a common thing? "Well, it is if you have cattle stolen; it is just a small part of the puzzle. We are doing the investigation, so we have discretion as to who should be notified. I suppose we must leave as soon as possible," said #47. "Yes, but we can stop anyplace you want to get some rest; we have been going nonstop it seems," replied #43. "Is it possible to contact these two witnesses?" asked #47. "I think it is a little too soon; we should wait until we get into Colorado, and besides, we need to rest our brains and body first," replied #43.

Jace Honey grew up around cattle his whole life; he was a hard-working rancher and had been able to become part of the family run business. His family had started The La Junta Livestock Commission in 1955, which is still running strong. He is the president and

general manager now. He had his best friend Daryel McCurry working with him. They had been friends since they could walk, and now,
they had the best of both worlds doing what they enjoyed and being
married to their sweethearts. Most of the people that knew Jace would
kid him about robbing the cradle because his wife Lesli was so much
younger than he. He was known to be a family man and very giving.
His wife, Lesli, works in the front office and is very happy to be a part
of Jace's life. Daryel is married to Ronda. They got married the cowboy
way, on horseback; it was truly a beautiful ceremony. Daryel, being
a rodeo bronco-busting cowboy, finally had to change his ways due
to all the injuries he sustained, and settle down to buying and selling
cattle. They both were the real-deal; grown-up cowboys, still living life
to the fullest. That all changed two weeks ago, when Daryel and Jace
were together checking on a herd of cattle to be auctioned at the stock
yards. The owner had left word with Daryel to look at the cattle and
call him to see what the going price would be for the cattle. Jace used
a pair of binoculars and looked over the cattle, when he watched five
trucks and two cattle trucks pull up to the far fence. Several men got out
and cut the fence. Two trucks drove in and started to drive around the
herd and gathered them toward the opening. One of the cattle trucks
let down the ramp and doors; the cattle had nowhere to go but inside
the truck. Daryel got out his 45-caliber pistol from under the seat and
said that he was going to stop the cattle rustlers, when Jace told him
to sit tight. The men had automatic rifles and had set up a perimeter
around some of the trucks. Jace watched as a group of women were
led from one truck to another; they were handcuffed and looked in
bad shape. A man with a pair of binoculars was looking around, when
he saw that they were being watched by Jace and Daryel. He spoke
to a man that held a rifle and he pointed it their direction. He fired
off twenty rounds into the air. He did not hit anything, but Jace and
Daryel got the message and left; their GMC tires threw up dirt as they
left. The rustlers sent two trucks to go after them, but Daryel knew his

way around and lost them on an old dirt road that went into a canyon; it was an old cowboy trick used to lose Indians and a good defensive tactic. They were not followed. They reported it to the State Police and Cattleman's Association. They got no response from State Police, so Jace used a few connections at the Governor's office to find someone to look into the incident.

A few days had passed, when Jace and Daryel heard the bad news; the rancher that had his cattle stolen was found dead, hanging from a tree in his own backyard with multiple gunshot wounds. This was the work of some very bad men and it shook the cattle community from all of the surrounding areas. There was a rumor going around that it was the work of the cartels out of Mexico; they were stealing cattle and females to ship into Mexico. The women would be used as mules to carry drugs to cross the border, and then gathered up again by truck. Some of the women tried to escape, but were caught, and the cartel forced them into prostitution, until they were no longer of any use. The amount of fentanyl that was coming across the border was making the cartel millions of dollars a day, and they were using that money to pay off U.S. Officials, every chance they could.

Jace and Daryel stayed close to work and home at the insistence of their wives. It seemed that most of the ranchers were packing heat and not afraid to show that they were armed. The Old West had returned to the cattle community and they were ready for a fight; one of their own had been killed by outsiders. Jace and Daryel knew that help was on the way, but they had no idea who or what agency was coming to investigate. They just had to sit and wait.

The trip to Colorado seemed longer than usual to #47, and she was glad that they stopped in Raton to rest up. #43 had gone over all the maps and information again, while she cleaned her gun and checked all of her equipment. #47 took the hint and did the same thing, and asked if she could make a call to the witnesses. #43 said, "Sure, and let them know that they will be on speaker phone and recorded. Let them know that we are the two investigators that are assigned to this case. We will get to the bottom of this crime, and justice will be brought to the individuals who are responsible. Our condolences to the family of the victim." "Got it," replied #47.

Jace and Daryel were at the stockyard when Jace received the call from #47. Everything seemed on the up and up, but Jace could not get a name from the caller and that was a red flag for him. They had all the information that Jace had given Senator James, so it was legit, but he still did not know what department was looking into the incident. The investigators wanted to meet them so they could possibly help them with the lay of the land in Colorado and cattle regulations. Jace was the man for that, and Daryel was his right-hand man who knew all the roads South of Denver and East, going into Kansas. It would be a few hours before the investigators showed up, so Jace and Daryel reviewed all the information they had, and laid it out on a desk for them. Jace told Daryel that the investigators did not have a clue about Colorado; they were from out of state, so do not get your hopes up.

When #43 and #47 showed up at the stockyards, they met Jace and Daryel. Jace and Daryel showed them some hospitality and offered them some coffee and a hand shake. #43 shook their hands with a firm grip and handshake. #47 grabbed Daryel's hand with a very firm grip and shook the big man's hand and did the same with Jace. Jace and Daryel were impressed with the grip of #47 and did not press either of them about their names; they just addressed them as madam, which sounded more like "Ma'am". #43 noticed that they both wanted to know their names, so she simply explained that they could not give them their names, due to the policies and procedures of their agency; but, rest assured, they would get to the criminals sooner rather than later. Jace and Daryel smiled and felt better about who they were dealing with, and continued to show them everything they had on the desk.

Jace explained that he had called State Patrol, but they never came out to investigate. #43 smiled and said, "We are going to be looking into that further down the road." #47 looked at Daryel and asked if he could put himself in the shoes of the rustlers to see where they might try to steal cattle again or where they would be able to leave an area undetected? Where would they pick up and drop off their female captives? Jace said he could make a few calls to some ranchers, to see if anyone had seen anything unusual around their properties. Daryel said that there was Hwy 350, just outside of La Junta, that would take you all the way to Trinidad and to Raton, New Mexico. That would avoid I-25 and State Patrol. Jace said that he thought that Colorado Springs, Pueblo, and Trinidad were the best bet for human trafficking, due to the size of the towns and the crime rate. Colorado Springs also had a large military presence. It was early afternoon when #43 stated that they needed to find a hotel for the next several days, and if Jace did not mind, they would like to use the stockyards as a home base during their investigation. Jace smiled and told them they could use the extra office in the corner of the room and that there was a Holiday Inn not far South on Highway 50. #47and #43 thanked them and told them they would be in touch.

Daryel stood next to Jace and asked him, "Did you feel the grip of that little lady, my God, she could rip the horns right off a steer." "Yes, I looked down at my hand and she left finger marks in my hand; she was all of 5'6" and 120 soaking wet," said Jace. "I don't think I would like to piss her off; something tells me she could be your worst nightmare." "You never have seen Ronda pissed off; hell has no fury like a woman scorned," said Daryel. "Yup, it's best to keep your woman happy, if you want to wake up in the morning," said Jace. They both laughed and said it was time to head home. Dinner would be ready by the time Jace got home, and Daryel still had some chores to do before he could relax.

#43 and #47 checked into their hotel. It was very comfortable and it fit their needs. #43 asked if #47 wanted to order in or go out for dinner. #47 said, "Order in." #43 turned around and said, "I'll see you in a few minutes and we will look at what we have to choose from around here." #47 unpacked her clothes and put them into a dresser drawer. She placed her shoes and boots on the floor; she wanted to feel normal and have everything in its place. When #43 came back into the room, she saw that #47 had laid out her clothes and boots. She had unpacked her bag, but everything was set up as if she were going to have an inspection, like in the military. "Wow, I've never seen anyone unpack and set everything out," said #43. #47 replied, "A student of mine used to say, "Always ready, Never surprised." "Mm-mm, I will keep that in mind," said #43. #47 told #43 that she was next to take a shower and she would be back so they could discuss what to order. #43 started to unpack her duffel bag of clothes and put some of them away, when she noticed that #47 had left room in the drawers for her. "How thoughtful of her." #47 came out of the shower, all dressed in black, with her hair pulled back. "That was fast. Are we ready to order?" asked #43. "We are; let's go down to the desk and ask them for some ideas of good food to order." #47 grabbed a light jacket and put on some black slippers. #43 grabbed her jacket and made sure she had the room key. She did a quick glance of the room before they left.

#43 was standing at the desk, talking to the manager about food, when a couple walked into the lobby from the elevators. There were two, short men who walked on each side of the woman; she looked down and had her hands in her coat. The woman asked one of the men if she could use the lady's room, and was denied by the man. #47 heard and saw what had happened and slowly walked towards the woman, watching the men on both sides of her. #47 told #43 that she had to use the lady's room and walked towards the woman and said, "Hey, I'm going to the lady's room and I need some company," as she grabbed the woman's arm. The man looked at her and said, "She doesn't have to go." #47 laughed at the man saying, "Mister, you have no idea what a woman needs or wants." She pulled the woman into the restroom.

#47 pushed the woman inside one of the stalls and told her not to move until she came back. One of the men started to open the door, when #43 said, "Hey you, that's the lady's room; the mens room is down the hall." The other man told #43 to mind her own business, as he pulled his coat off to the side, to show a gun in the waistband of his pants. #43 stepped towards him and said, "If you are going to show it, I hope you are ready to use it." The man grabbed his gun and #43 grabbed his hand so he could not pull the gun out. The man at the lady's room, opened the door and was met with a fist to the face, as she grabbed his shirt to pull him into another punch to the face. It happened very fast and the men were not ready to fight two women that were much more skilled than they were. The men wanted to retreat, but the women were relentless and continued to give them a beat down. #47 pulled the man into the lady's room and hit him in the throat with her fist; there was a crunching noise from his throat, as his face turned beet red and he fell to the floor, clutching his throat. #43 was hitting the man, with the gun, multiple times in the face and stomach; until he bent over and vomited on the floor. #43 took the man's gun, threw it aside, and checked him for identification. #47 opened the stall door for the woman and told her to hold her arms out. She looked at her wrists, and saw that they were black and blue from wearing handcuffs. #43 told the manager to call the police and say there was a human trafficking victim at her desk, and there were two men that needed medical attention. #43 asked the manager to use the phone. She picked it up and said she had an emergency call to make. "Yes, of course, please use the phone in my office," replied the manager. #47 looked for identification on the dead man and found money and a cell phone in his pockets. He had no I.D., but she took the gun that #43 had thrown aside. She took it apart and left it in pieces on the desk, after wiping it down. #43 came out of the office, smiled at #47, and said that everything would be taken care of, as they sat and waited for the police. The woman started to tell #43 and #47 that she was a mule for the cartels and there were several others in room #301. They are tied up and drugs are in the brown bags in the bathroom. #47 said that everything will be fine, and everybody will be rescued.

The police arrived, as well as ICE and the DEA. Several of them were wearing silver Lady Justice pins on their collars. The manager escorted the police and DEA to room #301. When the manager opened the door, she saw several women dressed only in panties and bras. They wore handcuffs; food bags and trash were on the floor and bed. The DEA found all the drugs in the bathroom with scales and plastic baggies. It was a good bust; over thirty pounds of fentanyl and ten pounds of marijuana. The women were taken to the hospital to be checked out and would later be interviewed by the DEA and ICE. There was one man, who was DOA, due to a crushed larynx. The other man was treated for minor injuries and would recover.

After the police, ICE and the DEA left the lobby and all the transports were done, #43 smiled at the manager and asked, "Where were we, before we were so rudely interrupted?" #47 said, "Food, we need some food!" The manager smiled and said, "I got this, it's on the house." As she flipped her collar over to show them a Lady Justice pin. As #43 and #47 walked away, #47 asked, "How many people have those pins?" "I don't know; I just know that there is always help close by and know that there are only a few of us that leave "Justice Served" cards."

The hotel manager went to their room and delivered their food on a small cart. On it, was a large Godfathers Pizza, a bottle of red wine and two pints of pistachio ice cream. A small card was left near the wine saying, "Thank You for your service. Mr. Jefferson." They ate dinner and watched the local News at Nine. The news anchor stated that a sting operation took place in La Junta, where two men were part of a drug ring trying to sell drugs out of a local hotel and they had rescued several women from human traffickers. During an altercation, one man died of his injuries and another was treated for minor injuries;

no police were harmed and the investigation is still on-going. #43 and #47 had a good laugh before saying good-night.

A good night's sleep was interrupted by a phone call from the manager's desk saying she would be at their door in two minutes to relay an urgent message left by Jace Honey. It was eleven-thirty at night, and #43 did not remember telling Jace where they were staying.

The manager was met at the door by #43 and was told that Jace had called three hotels with the same message. "If there are two female investigators staying at your hotel, tell them to come to my office. Daryel is in Outlaws Canyon, hiding from the cartel; it's an emergency, he's been shot." The manager told #43 that Outlaws Canyon was on private property and it was at least a good thirty minutes away. #43 turned to see that #47 was on the phone, already talking to Jace. #43 got dressed in brown and black camouflage and put on her holster. When #47 finished talking, #43 was ready to leave. #47 talked while getting dressed; she wore all black with a hood and carried her two knives and a short sword to include throwing stars. #43 asked, "No gun?" #47 looked puzzled and said, "Thanks, I almost forget my weapon of choice, when working at night." #47 went into the bottom of her black bag and put together her bow and arrows to put into a small leather pouch and tied it around her neck and back. #47 walked passed #43 and asked if she was going? #43 smiled and said, "Let us find this party and spread some cheer; Jace is waiting for us."

Jace was waiting at his truck; it was running. He had a 30-30 Winchester rifle in his hand and a first aid box in the other. #43 and #47 pulled up to Jace's truck and got in, not saying anything. He looked at them and was a little taken back to see two women looking for a fight. Jace talked while driving, and hit a dirt road throwing up gravel as the truck slid into a curve. Jace slowed down just long enough to hear gun fire as he got close to where Daryel was hiding. #47 went out of the truck window, feet first, saying to #43 not to worry about her. She would follow the gun fire. #43 did not have time to say anything; #47 was gone, like a ghost in the darkness. Jace stopped the truck and got out and started to look for Daryel when #43 grabbed him by the collar and told him to sit still next to the truck; he was not to talk or shoot at anything. Jace saw that #43 meant what she said, and sat down on the ground next to the front wheel. #43 had her gun at the ready and listened to talking in the distance. The cartel had flashlights and were sweeping the dirt road leading into the canyon looking for Daryel. #43 watched the lights getting closer. There were five of them, and #43 had her sights on the lead flashlight. The men were talking and their voices carried in the dark night; they were trying to scare Daryel, by saying that they were going to cut him up for the coyotes. Jace watched as the lights got closer and he grabbed his rifle. #43 had turned to him and wagged her finger at him, as if he had been bad. Jace put his rifle down and nodded his head. The cartel men were laughing and said that they would find him soon and they would show him mercy if he showed himself now.

Without any warning, the lead man was hit with two arrows to the chest and went down, shining his flashlight on the others walking near him. One of the men started to say something, but the sound of multiple thuds of arrows hit him in his chest and put him down. Another man started to shoot his automatic rifle spraying bullets into the surrounding bushes and darkness. The other men panicked and shot into the darkness, and yelled about killing Daryel. The shooting stopped, one by one, as #47 used her short sword to cut them into pieces. They were screaming for their lives, not understanding what was going on, as they lost an arm or hand, and finally their heads. #47 walked slowly down the road, saying it was all clear. Daryel came out, only ten feet away from where #47 was standing. He had seen and heard a lot of the killing that had taken place. Daryel had a gunshot wound to the right leg; the bullet went through his upper thigh. Looking at Jace he said, "They shot me in my good leg, damn it." "I didn't think you had a good leg to start with. Do you need medical?" asked Jace. Daryel looked at Jace and told him, "Thanks for the concern, and yes, I need medical!" Jace put his arm around Daryel to help him take the weight off his leg and helped him into the truck. #43 looked at #47 as she walked to the truck. #47 asked #43 if she had any "Justice Served" cards. #43 smiled and said, "Of course, we are on mission." #47 walked back to the bodies and put cards into the dead men's mouths as she retrieved her arrows. The ride back into town was slow, and Jace wanted to clear the air by asking why he was not allowed to help? #43 told him that they were to keep all civilians safe, at all costs, without exception. Jace asked why they did not call the police? #43 answered, "This was a mission to save your friend's life; would you or Daryel like to explain to the authorities what you were doing, and why the cartel was involved, instead of leaving it up to the professionals?" "We were just trying to help." said Jace. "I know that, but do you think, for a minute, that the cartels are going to stop? We just put the fear of God into them; they do not know who or what hit their team. All they know, is that a calling card was left in the mouths of five dead men. You, my friends, are now out of the picture; we want to thank you for your help and please do not talk about this event. It would only come back and bite you in the ass. It would really piss off my friend, and you would not want to piss her off now, would you?" said #43. Daryel looked at Jace and shook his head, knowing what #47 could do; having seen firsthand the speed and deadly nature of the little lady that had the strength to crush your hand if she had wanted. Jace dropped the women off at their hotel and continued to the hospital. He knew that they would just be in the way, from this point forward. Daryel looked at Jace and asked, "How am I going to explain this to Ronda? She is going to have my ass." Jace laughed, and told him to tell the truth. He said that, "It was the better part of valor, and, oh, by the way, I called her already; that is what friends do." When they got to the hospital, Ronda was waiting for them at the emergency room with the doctors.

#43 and #47 knew the mission was far from over, but now they would not have to watch over two cowboys that were meant for better things with their wives. #47 told #43 that she was going to have to get out more and see what real crime was lurking in the shadows of the Old West. What bothered #43 was the information they received about how China had made their way into every aspect of American society and they were not acting alone. The Mexican Cartels were controlling everything from the border states to Chicago with the drugs and gangs. #47 wondered how a few Justice Seekers are going to make a difference in such a big country; they would need a lot of help. #43 and #47 both had to make some adjustments to the mission, after talking with Mr. Jefferson and advising him of the turn of events at Outlaws Canyon. They were going to follow the trail left behind by the cartel, and see where it leads them. Mr. Jefferson told them that he was working with a couple out of Colorado, who had not yet finished with their training; but they would be ready soon. Mr. Jefferson had asked them if they needed some R & R before their next phase of the mission. #43 and #47 both declined the R & R, and wanted to get down to business. But, they did ask for a training area with a shooting range. Mr. Jefferson told them that he had a place in mind. It was near Barstow, California. He would send them the information if they wanted to go. #47 stated that she wanted to go. #43 laughed at #47 saying that she thought that they had just taken the bait; Mr. Jefferson wanted us to be there for the next phase of our mission. #47 said, "Mr. Jefferson would have made a great war general." #43 responded saying, "What makes you think that he isn't?" "He is always three steps ahead of anyone. So, what do you think we will be doing in Barstow?" asked #47. "Well, we took a pass on the R & R, so who knows; we'll just have to wait for our instructions," said #43. We must pack and get on the road. We must buy some new clothes and I need a computer to look up some information. "Having a computer isn't secure; we need Mr. Jefferson to give us a direct line to him. We should ask for permission, not beg for forgiveness," said #47. "You are right, we will buy new clothes," replied #43.

11

WELCOME TO MARINE BASE YERMO, MA'AM

THREE HOURS LATER, #47 said that she would have to buy another duffel bag so she could fit all her new clothes in it. #43 reminded her that Barstow was hot and she would be thankful for all the new clothes. The drive to California was long and they played mind games of "What If Scenarios" and found a few hole-in-the-wall places to eat. They got pulled over by State Police as they entered the State of Nevada. The officer was very nice and showed them his Lady Justice pin. He said that he had a package for them from Mr. Jefferson. He told them to drive safely and buckle up. They thanked the officer and continued on their way. As #47 started to open the package, #43 told her to wait until she was able to pull over. They both wanted to know what he had in store for them. Inside the package, were two cell phones that were encrypted with a biometric lock on them; they could not be hacked or used by anyone but the user. They also had new drivers' licenses and Identification paperwork, so they could enter Marine Corps Base Yermo as martial arts instructors. They would stay in Officer's Quarters, as a guest of the Quartermaster General. They even had orders from the Secretary of Defense to train soldiers to improve their combat readiness. #43 told #47 to be ready to be called Ma'am all the time, and they will not have a name while on base. "I grew up in a military family; just make sure you always have your I.D hanging from your neck; you may be checked until everyone gets used to you. By the way, you got your training area and I got my shooting range. I am so glad that I bought three sets of workout cloths," said #47. #43 laughed and apologized, saying, "Sorry, we will be wearing our traditional Karate GI, or in your case, a Chinese Kung fu or Shaolin uniform. We will be true warriors on the mat and train them to the best of our ability, without exception to rank." #47 smiled and said, "This should be fun." #43 said, "You have no idea; there will be a lot of men in uniforms, and they like to wear green yelling "sir, yes sir" or "sir, no sir." There is a rank structure from private to general and we need to know who we are talking to, so start reading. The day will start with reveille, and then the soldiers will do some sort of physical training (PT). After that, the raising of the flag, when everyone will stop whatever they are doing, to include driving. Then, you will stand next to your car and face the flag, at attention; if you are a soldier, you will salute. If you are a civilian, you will stand at attention with your hand over your heart. The morning breakfast is chow, as are all meals; you eat at a Mess Hall. There is no breakfast in bed. Officer's Mess serves better food, so be happy. The work day ends around five o'clock and taps are at nine P.M., which means the start of quite time. The few people you want to know, are the people in charge, like the Sergeant Major or Master Sergeant. All sergeants are not equal; count the stripes and learn their titles. My favorite was getting to know the Gunnery Sergeant at the mess hall. He could really hook you up with some good food. I do not know how long we will be training the troops, but try to know the guards at the gates; they can be helpful. The head-honcho of the Military Police, is the Provost Marshal; he or she will be the big dog in charge of the police (MP). If I'm going too fast, let me know so I can repeat myself and if you have any questions, let me know." #43 looked over at #47 to see that she was sound asleep, saying, "Huh, my ex did the same thing every time we went on a long drive; it must be the motion."

It was a long drive, and #43 needed to stretch her legs. She was hungry so she woke #47 and told her it was time to eat. #47 asked, "Are we there yet?" #43 shook her head and smiled, it was classic. "No, but I can eat; how about you? "Sure, just tell me where we are going; I could eat anything." replied #47. #43 asked, "What does your stomach say, or should I ask if you have any gut feeling?" "I'm good, just hungry." replied #47. A large sign said Welcome to Las Vegas, as they entered the city limits. It was hot and there was a lot of traffic. #47 asked if it is always this hot in Las Vegas? #43 told her that this was normal, day or night; the city that never sleeps, "What happens in Vegas, stays in Vegas", so the saying goes. We need gas very soon"; the GMC had a large gas tank and it was now on one-eighth of a tank. As they pulled into a small gas station, they saw that there was a taco shop in half of the gas station. #43 said, "Good, we can kill two birds with one stone." #47 asked, "Is that a thing in Las Vegas?"

#43 looked at her and asked, "What?" "Having a gas station/taco shop," replied #47. "It makes sense here; who am I to judge?" #43 started to pump the gas while #47 walked inside to pay the cashier. Inside, she could smell the tacos filling the air. There was a line at the order counter and a line at the cashier's; she told the cashier that she wanted one-hundred on pump #3 and gave her the money. The cashier gave her a receipt, without looking up, and said the line for tacos is on your right, next to the restrooms. #47 saw the line, snake around a table and got in line. She noticed that people were buying tacos by the bagful; the line moved fast, so she looked at the menu and saw tacos with every ingredient. #43 walked in looking for #47, when #47 started to wave her hand. #43 saw that tables were at a premium and told #47 to get them to go; get any kind you want as they are all good. #43 went back to park the truck and waited for #47 to come out. It was twenty-minutes later when #47 came out smiling with three bags in her hands, saying that she scored. #43 asked, "How many tacos did you get?" "I got twenty tacos with sides of rice and beans" All #43 could do was laugh and say, "I know I'm hungry, but you must be starving." #47 told her that she had never heard of some of the ingredients and wanted to try them. #43 wanted to know what kind of tacos she got and looked inside the bags to find the receipt showing carnitas, beef tongue, al pastor, steak, lamb barbacoa, birria and carne asada. After looking at the receipt, she told #47 she was now starving and wanted to eat now in the truck. #47 smiled and said, "See, I told you so; I'll get us some drinks." #47 went back inside and came out with two large horchata drinks, saying, "It's a rice drink." #43 laughed and said, "Yes, it is a rice drink; you don't get out much, do you?"

They sat in the parking lot of the gas station in taco heaven. Neither of them wanted to move; there were two tacos and untouched rice and beans left. #47 saw a homeless man begging for food or gas money and told #43 that she was not going to waste the food and wanted to give it to the man. #43 smiled and told her to do whatever makes her feel good. #47 gave the food to the man who thanked her several times and even bowed to her. #47 bowed back and got into the truck saying, "Now we are ready to drive and let us get there before dark, or at least, let's make a good try at it." #47 smiled and said, "Want me to drive?" "No," replied #43, "we would get pulled over for sure; you can barely see over the steering wheel and we do not need any attention. #47 looked at #43 and there was silence for about a minute. #43 smiled and said, "Just kidding, I love this truck and the way it handles; you can go back to sleep if you want. I will put the music on low for you. #47 just looked out the window seeing what Las Vegas looked like in the daytime. #47 thought about home, or what home used to be, before she met Mr. Jefferson. It was true that she didn't get out much and she missed seeing her mother and eating her mother's traditional food. She wanted to train and find the Triad leader and kill him. It was getting to be the time for the Festival of the Dragon and she always knew when it was near. #47 also wanted to test #43 on the mat; after all, she had trained under her grandfather, had showed that she had good training under his guidance. But she did not know how much of the Black Dragon techniques she knew; a test was coming, and it wasn't personal; it was professional.

It was late afternoon, when they reached the access road leading to Marine Base Yermo. It was in the middle of nowhere and Barstow was the nearest town thirteen miles to the West. The road was two lanes in, and two lanes out of the base, with a long chain link fence stretching for miles across the road with a two-man guard station that controlled the gates that crossed both lanes. A Marine guard stepped out and looked at their vehicle that had no military stickers on the window. He waved them to an area to be searched and to sign in and show their orders. #43 pulled over and got all of their paperwork and vehicle registration out and told #47 to put her I.D around her neck. #43 did the same as the MP looked at all the paperwork. The MP made a phone call to the Base Commander and said, "Yes sir" several times before he hung up the phone. The MP turned to face #43 and #47 and said, "Welcome to Marine Base Yermo, Ma'am; the base commander requested that I escort you to his quarters. I have two maps of the base and I will highlight the roads and area that you will be training in; if you get lost for any reason, please call this number and an MP will assist you to find your way around." "Excuse me sir, is there any place where I can freshen up before we leave?" asked #47. "Mam, I am Sergeant Thomas. I am not an officer; the head is round the corner and I will wait for you. #43 looked at #47 and told her the restroom is around the corner. #47 said, "Sorry". #43 addressed Sergeant Thomas and said that her friend had never been on a military base before, but she is a quick study. Sergeant Thomas smiled and said, "Yes, Ma'am." When

#47 showed up, they got back into the truck and #43 put a temporary vehicle tag in the left side of the window, as requested. The MP started driving slowly, but got up to speed as there was little to no traffic. The ride was just a few miles away, but it seemed longer as they stopped in front of officer's quarters and the base commander's billet.

A short man in a tan uniform stood by waiting for them. He had a red face from being outside, but you could see the tan line on his scalp. He was not fat, but stocky with a big chest and had a smile that lit up his face with white teeth. He had one star on his collar and #43 quickly told #47 that he was a general and she knew him; he was one of her father's old friends from back in the day. #47 smiled and said, "Got it." "General Taylor, how are you doing? It has been years since I have seen you and I thought that you retired years ago." said #43. "Grace, great to see you. Well, I tried twice, but the brass kept offering me a promotion to stay, so here I am, until you and your partner in crime, finish up here with your orders from the top. After my final report to the Defense Department about our combat readiness, I am submitting my papers again, this time for good." #47 bowed to the general saying, "I am Sensi Katsumi, here to train your Marines to the best of my ability to ensure that they are combat ready; it is my pleasure to meet you sir," as she extended her hand." The general shook her hand and smiled. "It is my honor to have you here to train my men. Thank you, Ma'am."

#43 saw how #47 handled herself and she felt as if she had been played. There was more to her than meets the eye; she was professional and polite, but very deadly. #43 knew it was part of her persona she had been trained in the old ways. #43 was mad at herself for not checking the I.D. badges closer. The general made small-talk and showed them their quarter and gave them the directions to the Mess Hall and the gymnasium. He said that training starts at eight sharp. It was time to turn in and they both were ready to get some rest; well, at least #43 was ready. She had been driving all day while #47 took cat-naps. Not much was said between them that evening; it had been a long day. #47 had several papers she was going over and did not even bother to unpack. Instead, she sat on the floor at a coffee table and started to read everything she had on Marine Base Yermo Annex. The base was just over two-thousand-square acres and served as a storage, distribution and maintenance depot for the United States Marine Corps, employing about two-thousand-five-hundred people. It was the railways that made it so important, going North into California. #47 heard the bugle over the loud speakers; it was taps. It sounded sad and yet peaceful; it was quiet time on the base. #47 sat on the floor, her legs crossed and her hands on her thighs, holding her forefinger and thumb together. She went into a deep meditation recalling what #43 had said about the Marines on base.

The day started just as she remembered, with reveille. She woke up #43 and told her she was going for a run before chow. Before #43 could say anything, she had gone out the door. Running in between two white lines, she followed a small group of Marines running and singing a cadence which was sort of fun, but they ran too slowly for her, so she ran past them. #47 saw a large field where another small group of Marines were doing push-ups and climbing ropes. #47 got down and did fifty push-ups, ran to the ropes and waited until there was an open spot, then jumped up to grab the rope before anyone else could. She climbed the rope faster than a monkey to the top, where she pulled herself up and walked the wooden beam to the other rope, slid down and faced the ground as if it were child's play, leaving the Marines watching with their mouths open. It was a great display of speed, strength, and balance. As she left the area, she heard several Marines yell, "OOHRAH!" #47 was running back, when an MP pulled up alongside her in his patrol vehicle. It was Sergeant Thomas, from the gate. #47 stopped running and listened to what the Sergeant had to say. "Ma'am, I received a report of a civilian that ran through the ranks of a formation and disrupted a platoon of Marines doing PT. Was that you Mam?" #47 replied, that she was setting an example for the Marines to adapt, improvise and overcome. Sergeant Thomas looked at her and said, "OOHRAH, Ma'am, have a nice day."

#43 was waiting for #47 at the Officer's Mess Hall. She was visibly upset with #47, as she walked through the doors. #47 greeted #43 and told her that she had a good workout and that she should join her next time. #43 responded saying that she would have joined her, had she waited for her to get dressed. "Sorry, I really didn't want to wake you, knowing how tired you were from driving all day yesterday," replied #47. #43 looked at #47 and told her that they would take it to the mat before eight or after five, take your pick. "I know what you are doing. Do not think for a second that I do not understand about your deception practices or your training," said #47. She took an orange and a banana with a bagel and cream cheese from the breakfast bar and told #43 that she would be waiting at the gym. "Fine," said #43, as she grabbed a bottle of water and an apple. She stormed out of the mess hall with her gym bag. #47 was waiting in the center of the mat when #43 arrived; it was seven-fifteen and #47 was already warmed up and walking in small circles, dressed in black from head to toe. #43 was dressed in her Karate GI and took off her shoes as she entered the mat. They met in the center and bowed at each other. #43 asked, "Rules?" #47 wagged her finger at her saying, "Only until you yield." That really pissed #43 off saying, "Fine, have it your way." They faced each other and #43 took a fighting stance. #47 was moving around her in small circles, like a cat. #43 kicked out and threw a punch. Then, she used a spinning back kick; all missed their mark. #47 moved side-to-side and gave a fake move to throw #43 off balance. On her next move, she jumped up in the air and did a spinning kick to her head. She missed with one foot, but connected with the other; hitting #43 in the shoulder and knocking her off balance. #43 did three spinning moves and tried to kick or punch #47. Then she did a cart wheel to avoid #47's next move. #47 made a fake jump move towards #43, but instead, moved to a sliding move, like a baseball player stealing second base and knocked #43 off both feet. #43 nodded her head saying, "Nice move," as she tried a flying superman to punch #47. It did not go well for #43, as #47 slid under her and kicked her in the back, knocking her to the mat. Now, #47 stood a few feet from #43 and started to move like a boxer; bobbing and weaving with her hands up. #43 started to spin in circles towards #47 and then jumped into the air over her head and hit her with a spinning kick, which knocked her to the mat. #47 rolled over, as she quickly recovered and went back into the boxing stance. #43 smiled as she tried to kick and punch her way towards #47. #47's timing was perfect. #43 threw a punch, and #47 half-turned and grabbed her arm, and swung her leg up and over #43's arm. Then she climbed on #43 and put her in a sleeper hold. #43 struggled and went to her knees. Her face turned beet-red and with moments from passing out, she tapped out. #47 helped #43 to her feet and asked if she was alright. #43 looked at her and told her that she was sorry for belittling her and it would never happen again. #43 asked #47 if she could ask one question of her. #47 said, "I know what you are going to ask and the answer is yes; I completed all the training." #43 bowed from the hip and showed respect, as she put one hand over the other saying that she was honored to be with her as a Justice Seeker.

It was seven forty-five when the first Marine showed up, as others hurried to get inside the gym. There were thirty Marines, all dressed in camo green as they sat on the edge of the mat with their boots off. Half of them looked eager to be there and the other half looked bored. #43 knew that this was the way it was most of the time for training, as she walked to the middle of the mat. #43 yelled, "Marines, stand up! You may call me Ma'am, from this point forward. But, you will address her as Sensi Katsumi", as #43 pointed to #47 and bowed. "We are here to test your combat readiness per the Department of Defense. Leave your attitudes at the door; you are here to learn new skills and refresh your old ones. Before we start training, we will warm up while we wait for the EMTs to arrive." The Marines were stretching and swinging their arms in circles until the EMT's showed up a few minutes later. #47 walked towards the Marines that were standing in two rows. #47 looked at the Marines that were there, because they had to be there, and asked, "Who wants to be here? Step over here," as she pointed to the right; "Those of you who want to leave, step over here," as she pointed to the left. There were five Marines that were on the left. She asked them to walk to the center of the mat and told them that if any of them could hit her, they could all leave; but, if they all hit the mat, they would have to stay and train with the others. "Ma'am, that would not be fair," said a Marine. #47 looked at the Marine and said, "I will keep my word. You are right; it isn't fair. There should be more of them; are there any volunteers?" Nobody moved, and now the Marines in the center of the mat felt a bit apprehensive. #43 stood several feet away and told them not to hold back, and fight. #47 did a cartwheel and kicked two of them to the mat. Then she jumped into the air and came down behind another two and hit them alongside their necks which knocked them out. There was just one Marine left and he smiled and saying, "I know how to fight and I won't hold back Ma'am." #47 looked into his eyes and walked up to him as he tried to hit her several times. Each time, #47 dodged and weaved and the Marine said, "All I have to do is hit you, right?" as he tried to kick her several times and then punch her. #47's timing was spot on and grabbed his wrist, twisted and turned it until she flipped him over her shoulder. The Marine hit the mat hard, as everyone could hear his breath leave his body. The EMT's ran to the Marine. He was alright as he looked up at his opponent, and she said, "That would be Sensi Katsumi from now on, Marine."

#43 stood in the center of the mat and told the Marines that the first lesson was over. She then requested that they tell her what they saw and learned. One Marine stated, "Never underestimate your opponent and give respect." Another Marine stated, "There is always someone who knows more than you, and be ready to fight." Another Marine stated, "Be willing to watch and learn because your life could depend on it." Sensi Katsumi smiled and told them that they were all good observations and answers. She said, "My question is, what could have turned the tide in your favor?" Nobody said anything at first, and then a voice came from the back saying, "If they had worked together when facing their opponent." #43 said, "Give that man a cigar." Sensi Katsumi smiled and said, "Adapt, improvise and overcome." All the Marines stood up clapping and gave a "OOHRAH!" #43 and #47 stood next to each other and gave a small bow to the Marines. They had a passing grade by the Marines, and they now had their attention.

It was time to see what the Marines were made of, as #43 asked if there were any weapons nearby? They stood around looking at each other and said, "No Ma'am." #43 asked again, "What would you do in combat?" "Remember, Marines improvise," said Sensi Katsumi. Several Marines ran and got three push brooms and unscrewed the handles from the brush. Another got a mop and took off the handle from the mop head, and another Marine grabbed a steel dust pan. "Well done," said Sensi Katsumi. Now, you five show me how you would use those items as weapons. Four of the Marines used the wooden handles as staffs and the fifth marine held the metal dust pan at his side using it as a short blade; keeping control of it as he swung it from side to side. Marines, this is a practical exam. "Use your heads!" shouted #43,"Everyone here, has a weapon on their person." A group of Marines got that "aha" moment on their faces as they took off their belts and wrapped them around their fist. A couple of Marines took off their t-shirts and rolled them up snapping them like a towel. "Well done," said #43, "Now we are thinking outside the box."

"At this time, please get dressed and observe, as we show you what can be done with those items. This is going to be a demonstration of what you can do with training." The Marines hurried up and sat in a large circle with #43 and Sensi Katsumi standing in the middle. #43 and Sensi both held a wooden handle and used them as a staff. They both bowed to each other and got into their fight stance.

Sensi Katsumi held her staff behind her and #43 held her broom stick out as if it were a sword, and held it with both hands. The Marines heard the staff going through the air; it was a blur. Sensi was twirling it so fast they couldn't keep track of it. #43 struck several times; the sound of wood hitting wood rang through the air. The skill that was demonstrated was beyond comprehending, which ended with Sensi vaulting over #43 and hit the staff from her hands. #43 rolled and picked up another staff, slid the dust pan handle on the end and stomped on the dust pan handle which secured it to the wood. #43 held the middle of her weapon and spun it around in circles with both hands. Sensi saw the weapon and broke her handle in half, holding a stick in each hand; it was a fighting style from Thailand. The style was very effective against the dust pan/staff. At times, #43 came within inches of cutting Sensi with the dust pan, but the sticks hit the pan several times with a rhythm. It was at this time, that Sensi started to turn in small circles spinning around so fast she became a blur, but the sound of the sticks was heard hitting the dust pan and wood. Finally, the wooden staff that #43 held broke. #43 took off her belt and started to snap it out at Sensi and then wrapped it around her hands with a long enough loop to catch the sticks and tie them up which made them useless. Sensi stood without any weapons and looked at #43 and bowed. #43 had won that round. The Marines went crazy, shouting and clapping.

#47 said, "This demonstration was to show you how, in your words, adapt, improvise, and overcome, are a reality with quick thinking and immediate action; never taking your eye off your opponent. This type of training will make you combat ready and give you confidence in your abilities. This is the end of day one. We have thirteen more days, Marines; we will see you on the obstacle in the morning. Do not be late." OOHRAH, Sensi Katsumi and Ma'am, OOHRAH", the Marines replied. The Marines sat on the mat and talked about the demonstrations as they put on their boots. Sensi Katsumi told #43 that tomorrow would be harder; they are going to show them new techniques, but show them the basic Judo, Krav Maga and Jujitsu and work from there. "Yes, Sensi Katsumi," as she smiled at #47. "Yes, you really won that last round; do not let it get to your head," replied #47.

The rest of the day was spent planning the remaining training courses for the Marines. There would be more groups to follow; the last, being the officers. #43 stated that she was going to advise Mr. Jefferson how things were going and would ask what their real mission was at USMC Base Yermo. She advised him that the Base Commander knew her from her childhood through her father. That was not a coincidence, she was sure, but would mention it anyway. #43 said that she was also going to call on Sergeant Thomas for a tour of the base. She wanted to see the railroad yards that went North and the rifle range. #47 thought it was a good idea and asked if she could join her. #43 said, "You do not have to ask; just be ready to go." "Always ready, Never surprised," replied #47. Sergeant Thomas returned #43's call about a tour of the base and said that he would have to make a few adjustments to his schedule, but would be happy to give them a tour. He asked if he could do it in the early evening so he could also finish a report on the railroad yard for the Base Commander. #43 was happy to oblige and asked if he had night vision glasses; if not, they had some and would be happy to bring them. Sergeant Thomas said it would be great because it would save time for him having to put in a request to get them from supply. Things were going smoothly for #43 and #47. It was a new experience for #47, as it gave her some insight to the workings of the military. After evening chow, #43 and #47 sat near their window waited for Segeant Thomas to arrive. It was just before dusk when he arrived, saying he was held up at the main gate with a few visitors. Sergeant Thomas asked to take #43's small duffel bag to the Humvee. "Sure," replied #43 and asked, "Why the Humvee; what happened to the jeep?" "I always use a Humvee when I go down range. Is it going to be a problem?" "No, we have never been in a Humvee before; it's kind of exciting." "Yes Ma'am; it can be," replied Sergeant Thomas.

"What are we going to see first; the range or the railroad yard?" asked #43. "Ma'am, we are going to the rifle range and pistol range first. I understand that it is on your schedule for the last day of training, am I right?" asked Sergeant Thomas. #43 said, "That is correct, Sergeant Thomas." The ride to the ranges was twenty-minutes and the drive was hot and dusty. #43 asked if she could stand in the gunner's hatch, showing Sergeant Thomas that she had military goggles in her hands already. "Yes Ma'am, thank you for asking and thinking about safety first; your eyes are very important." When #43 stood up, she was hit with a blast of hot air and sand hitting her face; maybe it was not such a good idea. Sergeant Thomas turned left on a smaller dirt road and turned a hard right and stopped. "Ma'am, we are here at range #12, used for rifles up to six hundred yards and the pistol range is a half a click away with a fifty-yard range. Were you looking for anything specific Ma'am?" "No Sergeant, this is good. I just wanted to get the lay of the land, so to speak. What are the rules before a range can go hot?" asked #43. "Well, Ma'am, the range instructor must be on the range and the medical team must be present. Range HQ must open the range, and lastly, all soldiers using the range must have gone through a range safety course before setting foot on the range. The red flag has to be up, showing a hot range," replied Sergeant Thomas. "Thank you, Sergeant, you seem to know your stuff." The Sergeant told them that he wanted to do his check of the railroad leading North. It will take thirty-minutes of driving and the dust is going to get very bad, so if you do not mind Ma'am, could you stay inside of the Humvee?" "No problem, Sergeant," replied #43.

It was twenty-minutes into the drive, when Sergeant Thomas slowed down and looked to the left. He saw a few flashes off in the distance, and then two bullets hit the driver's side window. Sergeant Thomas took evasive action and turned the Humvee away from the direction of the flashes. A few more bullets hit the side of the Humvee and Sergeant Thomas got on the radio to call the Military Police Headquarters to report that he was under fire from an unknown location from the North end of the railroad yard tracks. #43 told Sergeant Thomas to remain calm and to continue his evasive driving; but, weave your way towards the flashes. "Do what?" said Sergeant Thomas, "We have help coming and my job is to keep you civilians safe." "And you are doing a fine job; now make some dust and drive towards the flashes," replied #43. "Yes, Ma'am." Sergeant Thomas drove, making dust as he drove closer to the flashes; now being able to hear the rifle shots as he got closer. #47 had her night vision glasses on and said that it was one shooter, using cover next to the railroad. #43 told the Sergeant that she had an idea. She wanted him to shut off his lights and sit still. She said that the shooter was using the headlights to find his target, which was them. If they still get hits to the Humvee, then they will know that the shooter has night vision. Sergeant Thomas looked at #43 and told her that it was not a bad idea, but he didn't like not shooting back and would rather wait for back-up or just turn around. #43 told Sergeant Thomas that she had never heard of a Marine retreat. He gave a "Ooohrah" and stopped the Humvee. #43 was right; the shooting stopped. #47 told them that she was going out and run parallel to the railroad tracks to find the shooter. She had the advantage, by using night vision glasses. Before either of them could say anything, she was out of the Humvee in a dead run to the railroad tracks.

Sergeant Thomas looked at #43 and asked, "Who is that woman, they call Sensi?" "You wouldn't believe me if I told you; she knows combat on an entirely different level. Watch and learn," replied #43. Sergeant Thomas and #43 sat and waited for several minutes; it seemed like hours. Sergeant Thomas called the station and asked for an ETA of back-up. The reply was that they were en-route with the Base Commander and CID (Criminal Investigation Division).

#47 saw the shooter pack up his rifle and gear, and rolled it all up in a nice bundle. The shooter did not hear or see #47, as she stood behind him and watched him. "Going somewhere?" asked #47. The shooter turned to see a small female wearing night vision glasses. "Who the hell are you?" he asked. "Your worst nightmare," replied #47. The shooter pulled out his K-bar (Marine fighting knife) from his right side, and brought it up into his fight stance saying, "Sorry, nothing personal, but you are going to die tonight." "Any other time I would kill you, but tonight, I'm bringing you to justice," replied #47. The shooter did not waste any time and tried to stab #47 in the chest ,but she was not standing still long enough for him to get a good bearing. For his next move, the shooter swung his knife across his body several times, hoping to make contact, but missed. "You need better training; you will never kill me that way," replied #47, as she taunted him and made him madder by the minute. "I'm getting bored; I will stand still so you can stab me in my heart," as she pointed to her chest. The shooter moved fast with his knife, wanting to kill her. #47 turned her body as the shooter's arm passed by her and missed her. #47 grabbed his wrist and turned it in an upward movement, and locked his arm out. #47 hit his elbow, and watched it bend in the opposite direction. She heard the sound of the shooter who screamed in pain, as he dropped his knife. #47 had only dislocated it, but it was still painful as she hit him with the edge of her hand in a typical Karate move, knocking him out as it connected with his neck. #47 grabbed the solider by his shirt collar in one hand, and the bundle of gear in the other, and dragged him towards the Humvee. #47 yelled out to #43 and Sergeant Thomas that she had the shooter and to bring the Humvee; all was clear. When Sergeant Thomas pulled up in front #47, he shook his head and said, "Sensi, Ma'am, I have never witnessed such an act of bravery; to put oneself in danger the way you have." #43 gave Sergeant Thomas a nudge and said, "I told you so." Sergeant Thomas grabbed the solider to look at his name tag; it was Staff Sargeant Lopez. Sergeant Thomas knew of him; he was overly aggressive and had few friends. The MPs were now in sight and showed lights and sirens. #47 took the bundle and rolled it out to see a M-40A1 Remington 700 sniper rifle with a half box of ammo, in addition to a plastic bundle about the size of two bricks wrapped up with black duct tape. Sergeant Thomas saw it and told Sensi not to touch anything else. CID needed to see everything. Sergeant Thomas took out his handcuffs and put them on Staff Sergeant Lopez before he woke up.

The General and CID walked up to #43 and #47. They did not look happy, and they asked, "Grace, what the hell is going on here? If anything would have happened to you, it would have been my ass and I could kiss my retirement good-bye." "Sir, I can assure you, we are both fine. We were just along for the ride after seeing the rifle range per my earlier request, when we came under fire. Sergeant Thomas saved us by his driving skills." #47 gave #43 a nudge, and Sergeant Thomas smiled and told the Base Commander the whole truth to include Sensi jumping out of the Humvee and subduing Staff Sergeant Lopez by using night vision glasses and her martial arts skills. "Now that sounds like the truth to me; I want a full report on my desk before my coffee, is that clear?" replied the Base Commander. "Sir, yes sir." Sergeant Thomas replied, as he stood at attention and gave a salute. The General smiled and said, "Good work, and take these ladies back to their billet after they talk with CID." "Sir, yes sir," replied Sergeant Thomas.

It was almost one in the morning when they finished talking with CID and writing sworn statements. Poor Sergeant Thomas had to wait until everyone had their turn with CID, including himself. Reveille is coming early today and he was dreading it. #43 fell asleep on the couch and #47 did some meditation before she fell asleep on the floor. She woke up at reveille and woke #43 to ask if she was ready for a run. They both were dressed and out the door running, when twelve Marines joined them running towards the obstacle course, and another twelve Marines joined them half way to the ropes. It was amazing to watch twenty-four Marines running and climbing the ropes with new energy and determination not to fall behind. The Marines did not fail their instructors, as they all finished early. Somehow, the news had gotten out about #43, Sensi Katsumi and Sergeant Thomas; it was the talk during chow and all-around base, for that matter. A bad apple, by the name of Staff Sergeant Lopez was moving drugs for the cartels, using the railroad system going North. It was easy money, so he said. The drug was cocaine and fentanyl. He would put ten pounds in every tool box that was in each rail car that was going out every Tuesday. That was a total of fifty-pounds per week, for the last three months. Staff Sergeant Lopez would end up doing time in Leavenworth, under the UCMJ (Uniform Code of Military Justice), with a Dishonorable Discharge. The only good result to come out of this, was the amount of information he gave to CID about all his contacts in and around Barstow. The Base Commander had approval to have armed escorts for all the rail cars during movements going North. Drug dogs were doing searches for incoming and outgoing rail cars. Illegal drugs were becoming a big problem for all military bases with high volumes of traffic close to the cities and the border. The cartels had their hands into everything, to include human trafficking.

After chow, training that day went without any injuries. Several Marines found a new mission in life; to be better trained in martial arts. The routine of the training days became a blur with Marines doing PT in the mornings, and chow three times a day. "Sir, yes sir," or "Ma'am, yes Ma'am" became a regular thing to hear.Sensi Katsumi and #43 found a new respect and honor hearing taps at night, by standing at attention with their hands over their hearts and thinking about the sacrifice so many had given in the service of their country. #43 and #47 would go over Marine Corps history, after hours, to better understand the commitment of the Marines and what sets them apart from all others. It was simple, yet complex; God, Country, and the Marine Corps. The training days went by fast; the final class was with the officers on the mats, and the firing-range on the following day.

#43 and Sensi Katsumi stood in the middle of the mat and waited for the officers to enter the gym, but nobody entered. The sound of cadence was coming from the outside of the gym. There were thirty-six men, all dressed the same, with no insignia showing on their covers; they wore green t-shirts and green camouflage pants with black boots. As they entered the gym, they took off their boots and stood in a circle around #43 and Sensi Katsumi until everybody was inside and the doors were closed. A very large black man walked up to them in a military manner, with purpose and pride, and stood in front of them and shouted, "Officers of Marine Corps Logistics Base Yermo Annex are here to train with the instructors Ma'am." #43 and Sensi Katsumi smiled. Theses officers were ready; they had seen and heard of the talk and training of the previous week and the improvement of the morale of the Marines. It was their turn to show why they were officers. Sensi Katsumi walked in front of a Marine and asked him to state why this training was important to him. The Marine smiled and stated that he knew the disciplines of Krav Maga, Wing Chung, and Jujitsu but wanted to know more to pass on his knowledge to his men. Sensi Katsumi was surprised and bowed to him. She said, "Spoken like a true leader of men". The Marine bowed back and stood at the ready, in his fighting stance. Sensi Katsumi stepped back and went to another Marine and asked the same question. This time it went differently; the Marine did not smile, but just went into his fighting stance. Sensi Katsumi stepped back and said, "Whenever you are ready." The Marine went into a boxing style and then started to move from side-to-side. Then, he changed into Kung fu stance and waited for Sensi to make her move. Sensi Katsumi went high, spun in the air, kicked the Marine several times, and went low and deflected his kick. The next move was hard to describe, as Sensi punched and deflected all the moves the Marine had in his repertoire; the final move was Sensi putting him in a sleeper hold from behind. The Marine tapped out; stood up at attention and bowed towards Sensi Katsumi. "Never show or tell your opponent your skills until you are ready to use them; well done Marine." The morning and afternoon went by as each Marine showed their skill sets, with no injuries. It was a good day.

Range day, the last day of training, started at 0800 hours. They got an escort to the range, with all their gear by Sergeant Thomas in his Humvee. The Marines were already there, checking out ammo to load before the range instructor gave his safety brief. The flag was flying red and everybody was ready and groups were already formed. #43 and #47 were in the last group to fire. The range went hot. The first group stood in front of their targets; they went to their knees and then into the prone position. The same thing happened with group two and group three. #43 and #47 saw the same large black man walking the line barking orders. He was the Command Sergeant Major. Now, they had a title to the face. He was skilled and very formidable on the mat; he had the mindset to win at all costs. The last group finally arrived. As the Marines formed their line in front of their targets, the Command Sergeant Major barked the order that all civilians should step back from the line. #43 and #47 took a step back, as the Marines went through their fields of fire. #43 and #47 looked confused and wanted to shoot with the Marines. The Sergeant Major told #43 and #47 they did not have to shoot; it was only a requirement for all military personal to show their combat readiness. #43 asked the Sergeant Major for permission to speak. She was following military protocols; stood at attention, and showed him the respect he deserved. The Sergeant Major looked at #43. He knew who she was and said, "Permission granted." "Sir, Sensi Katsumi, and I would like to demonstrate the fine art of killing the enemy from one-hundred yards to fifty- yards, by using the weapons of our choice, that we have trained to use. The Sergeant Major looked down on the ground, and then looked up and said, "Permission granted". The Sergeant Major ordered all the Marines to sit in the bleachers and watch their instructors put on a demonstration of skill; shooting their weapons of choice.

#43 and #47 talked at the rear of the Humvee. #43 told #47 to give them a show that nobody will ever forget. #47 looked at #43 and told her that she had never fired a weapon before, but she did know how to take them apart. #43 told #47 to "think of the barrel as your finger, and when your slide locks to the rear, you are out of ammo and to reload and fire. The rifle is easy; point, aim and shoot. I will go first to show you, and you follow my lead." #47 put five of her throwing stars in her belt and took her wrist darts. They put on holsters with their Sig Sauer P-226 in 40 caliber with four extra magazines. Both carried an M-16 with two extra magazines.

#43 stood on the line and gave a nod towards #47 and the range master. An air horn sounded and #43 ran to the line and got into standing position with her rifle and shot until she had to reload. Then she went into the kneeling position, and shot until she ran out of ammo; then went into the prone, and shot all remaining rounds. #43 stood up and drew her weapon, as she walked slowly towards her target. When her slide locked to the rear, she knelt to reload and started to fire again. Then, she ran and shot to the left and to the right until she had to reload. She went into the prone and fired again, until she had to reload. While standing at the seven-yard line, she fired all of her rounds into the head of the target. #43 stood and faced her target, holstered her weapon, and put her hands up in the air. The range master walked up and took the target. There were whisperings in the bleachers and everybody wanted to see and hear the score.

The range master stapled the target to the target shack as he turned and smiled. #47 was next. As she walked to the line and bowed to the range master, the air horn sounded. #47 was on line and shot from the standing position, and slowly walked towards the target and knelt to reload. #47 started to shoot when she switched shooting from right hand to left. When she went to reload, she was in the prone shooting position again, but this time, she started to roll to the right while shooting. When she ran out of ammo, she stood and drew her Sig Sauer and fired at her target, running and rolling, showing the skill of a ninja. She did a cart wheel while shooting at her target, and stopped to reload while lying on her back; when the slide went forward, she shot her weapon while looking at the target upside down. It looked impossible; something out of Hollywood, but she made it look easy. As her slide locked to the back, she stood up and holstered her weapon. #47 was ten yards from her target when she spun around in circles and threw darts and stars at the target. When she finished, she stood still with her hands up, and turned around and bowed. The range master slowly walked to the target, and looked at it as he pulled it down. He took out the darts and throwing stars; they were in a small group where the head was supposed to be. The target had no damage except to the nine and ten rings. The range master took the target to the Sergeant Major and showed him Sensi Katsumi's target. The Sergeant Major turned and ordered that nobody is to touch the target; it is to be framed and hung in his office. The range master walked to Sensi Katsumi and told her that he had never seen anything like what he had just witnessed, and he gave her the throwing stars and darts. Sensi Katsumi held out her hand to show thanks. The range master took her hand and as she turned her hand upside down, a throwing star fell into his hand, as she told him to "never take your eyes off your enemy." The Sergeant Major had everyone come to attention before being dismissed and said, "Never in the history of the Marine Corps, have two civilians showed what it is to Adapt, Improvise and Overcome. We thank you both, for your instructions and due diligence to perform to the highest standards of the Marine Corps. Dismissed."

The end of the training schedule was at an end, and it was time to leave Marine Base Yermo. #43 and #47 were feeling kind of sad, but at the same time, happy to get on the road again. #43 turned to #47 and asked respectfully, "Was that the first time you ever shot a rifle or handgun? Because you really killed it out there. Honestly, I've never seen anything close to it, even in the movies." #47 looked at her and said, "That was the first time I ever shot a gun. I watched you shoot and I just wanted to try it, doing it in my own style. I honestly just did what you told me to do. Hey, you were the one that shot high expert for everyone to see. I was really impressed. So, how long have you been training with guns?" #43 smiled and said, "All my life; I started at the age of five with a BB gun. By the time I was twelve, I was shooting rifles with my dad." #47 said, "I have a question for you; is there some place on this base where a girl can get a drink?" #43 laughed and said, "I never would have expected something like that to come out of your mouth. What do you drink?" #47 said, "I don't know yet; I have to try a few drinks first to see what I like." "This is going to be fun; a girl's night out." said #43. "I have had plum wine and sake before, but that was ages ago. So, do we call a taxi or do we call Sergeant Thomas?" "That wasn't a question was it; we call Sergeant Thomas, of course. He's gotta hook a girl up sometime," said #43.

12

ALWAYS READY
NEVER SURPRISED

SERGEANT THOMAS WAS just finishing his shift when he answered the phone. He laughed and said that he would love to join them in a few drinks. He was off for the next three days. The question is, do you want to go to Barstow and get off base? #43 and #47 both wanted to get off base and they were ready to celebrate a mission completed. Sergeant Thomas told them that he would be at their billet in thirty minutes and to look for a black Jeep Rubicon. #47 told #43 that they should carry something for protection, as she showed her a small harness that went over her shoulders that hid two knives behind her back under her bra. "That is the coolest thing I ever saw; where can I get one? asked #43. "I custom made it years ago," replied #47. "I have these knife holders that attach to the back of my jeans when I wear this belt; the blades are about four and half inches long but they work. It's my version of conceal carry," said #43. They finished getting dressed and they looked each other over, giving each other a thumbs up. They were waited for Sergeant Thomas. The wait was not long when a black Jeep Rubicon pulled up. Sergeant Thomas was dressed in blue jeans and a white shirt with cowboy boots and black hat to finish his look. As Sergeant Thomas was about to knock on the door, it opened and the ladies ran to the Jeep calling shotgun. Sergeant Thomas held his keys in the air and said, "I'm driving." As Sergeant Thomas got behind the wheel, he said, "From this point forward, call me Jim. I am no longer on duty." "Roger that, Sergeant," was Sensi Katsumi's reply. This made #43 laugh. "So how may I address you?", as he looked at #43. "You may call me Grace, without the Ma'am." "You can call me Kat," said #47, from the rear seat. "Roger that, Sensi." Everybody laughed as Jim pulled away from housing.

First stop was a country western bar called The Trails End. It was part dance hall with pool tables on the upper-level, and there was a bar on both levels. The upper-level allowed people to watch the dancing by looking over the railing with small tables next to it. The music was loud and the place was crowded; the band was playing one of Charlie Daniel's songs, "The Devil Went Down to Georgia." "Hey Jimmy, glad you could make it, missed you last week."

The young lady was dressed in a tight form-fitting pair of blue jeans that showed every detail, and a loose-fitting blouse that hid her large, firm breasts. She had red hair that was pulled back into a ponytail with a million-dollar smile. Jim looked at Grace and Kat; his face was red from blushing, but he had a smile from ear-to-ear and told them that he had a girlfriend off base. Her name was Summer. Jim walked over to her and gave her a big hug, saying that he wanted her to meet the instructors that were on base for training. Summer was cute as she held Jim's hand and walked alongside him. Jim made the introductions, and everybody was ready for a round of drinks. Grace told Kat that she was having a Tequila Sunrise. Kat asked, "What is Tequila?" Grace explained that it was made from the Agave plant out of Mexico; it is a liquor normally served with salt and lime. "I'll try one," replied Kat.

Summer looked at Kat and told her that Jose Cuervo was no friend of hers; it made her crazy mad and she almost got thrown in jail for fighting. Jim came to my rescue and carried me away that night. Jim laughed and said, "Summer went from zero to sixty on the other woman. She never came back after that whooping." Kat looked at Grace and asked, "You think I'll be, OK?" "Sure, just do not mix drinks and stick to one shot per hour; be responsible. Besides, I got your back, so don't worry," replied Grace. "Who is going to have your back?" said Kat. "I got this; it is not my first rodeo and we have a DD (Designated Driver). What could possibly go wrong?" said Grace.

The night was slowly going by, and Kat and Grace were learning how to line dance with Summer and Jim. Jim asked Summer if he could teach Kat how to do the two step; it was out of respect to ask Summer. Summer liked that Jim was always thinking about her feelings. She was not the jealous type; besides, he was a very good dancer. Kat picked up the dance moves very fast and before she knew it, several cowboys asked her to dance. Grace watched Kat, like a brooding mother and smiled at each cowboy that held Kat. They were all gentlemen. Grace was surprised by a voice that came from behind her and asked her to dance, if she was not with anyone. Grace turned and smiled looking at a thin, young cowboy with a belt buckle the size of a small dinner plate. "Ma'am, my name is Buck, would you like to dance?" "Please call me Grace. Yes, I would love to dance with you." They walked out to the dance floor and waited for the next song to play; it was by George Strait, "I Cross my Heart." As Buck took her hand, Grace told him to keep one hand on her hip and the other hand in hers. Buck smiled and said, "Yes, Ma'am." As they danced, Buck sang along with the music. He sounded just like George Strait himself. Grace closed her eyes and moved with Buck; she was thunderstruck. She had missed the smell and gentleness of a kind man. When the song was over, Grace looked into Buck's eyes and she thanked him with a kiss on the cheek saying, "If you were ten years older, I'd run away with you." Buck's face turned red as he smiled and said, "If you don't mind waiting, I'll be here in ten years." Grace laughed and told him to find a young filly to dance with before she changed her mind. Buck tipped his hat, walked to the bar, and looked over his shoulder and smiled at Grace.

Summer walked up to Grace and said, "Girl, did Buck just rock your world or what"? That man has eyes for you and he is a good catch. "Yup, and he can sing as well as he dances," said Grace. Kat walked up to Grace and thanked her for the advice about drinking; she was on her eighth shot and was starting to feel light- headed. Grace told her to drink water and sit out a few dances until she felt better. Summer and Jim walked up to Kat and asked her if she wanted to step outside for some fresh air; it was getting warm and stuffy inside. Kat said that she would like that, as she walked towards the entrance with Summer holding her arm. "Jose Cuervo is no friend of yours honey, you best be careful. Some men are not gentlemen in these parts," said Summer. "You are with friends Kat, no worries,"said Jim. She was feeling high and was smiling the whole time.

Grace told Jim it was time for them to head home before she changed her mind and ran away with Buck. Jim and Summer laughed hard and said that they would have to rescue Buck from winning another belt buckle; hell, Grace would likely win a belt buckle. The group walked to the Jeep and got inside. Jim started the Jeep and asked, "Where to next?" Summer suggested they go to The Waffle House and have breakfast with Grace and Kat, to get some food inside them and waste some time. Kat said it sounded like a good idea, as she was hungry. Grace laughed and told them to keep their hands away from the table because Kat could really eat when she got hungry. They all started laughing; everyone was having a good time as Jim drove around looking for The Waffle House.

Jim saw the restaurant and pulled into the parking lot. There were a few cars and a panel truck with only a few people inside. They walked into the restaurant and sat in a corner booth. They could look out the window to see the Jeep parked under the lamp post. Grace thought that Jim had good situational awareness; always knowing his surroundings. He was always a gentleman to Summer. A waitress came to the booth with water and asked if they were ready to order. Kat asked to have another minute, as she was still looking over the menu. Summer said she was ready to order with her usual grits and coffee. Jim said he was having the eggs, bacon and a side of pancakes. Grace said that she was having the midnight special, whatever that was. Kat said that she wanted to try grits, but also wanted to have the Texas Beacon Cheesesteak Melt with hash browns and a waffle with ice tea. "That's my girl," said Grace. Everyone at the table laughed, "The little lady has an appetite; nothing wrong with that," said the waitress, as she walked away. The food arrived, and their table looked like a buffet with all the food spread out. Kat was eating like she was starving; Grace told the group that Kat's mother told Kat to always listen to her feelings and never ignore her stomach. "That is some sound advice if you ask me," said Summer. Jim also agreed saying that nobody does well on an empty stomach; ask any Marine. After they finished eating, Kat was feeling much better and everyone agreed it was time to call it a night. Grace took the check from Jim saying it was ladies' night and paid the bill. Kat said she was ready, but wanted to visit the lady's room before they left. Summer said that she would go with Kat. Jim and Grace sat at the table making small talk, when they heard Summer screaming. Jim got up and ran to the back hallway where the restrooms were located. The back door leading to the parking lot had been propped open. Summer was holding onto the door and kicking at the two men that were trying to grab her and take her to the panel van just outside the door. The men saw Jim, but they were still trying to grab Summer. She was putting up a good fight. One of the men took out a gun from his pants and held it at Jim's face. Before Jim could do anything, Grace had run around the building to the van, took her knives out and cut the tires of the van.

Then she went to the man with the gun. Jim was holding his hands up and saw that Grace was standing behind the man with the gun. She was holding a knife to his throat. Summer took a swing at the man as she let go of the door; her fist hit him right in the eye. Summer took advantage and kicked him between the legs, connecting with his "family jewels"; the man went to the floor. Grace had taken the gun away from the man, but still had a knife to his throat; his eyes wide open looking at Grace. Jim held Summer and asked if she was alright; she was trembling as he held her. Kat came out of the restroom with knives at the ready; it surprised Jim and Summer. Kat ran to the van door and heard someone pounding the sides of the truck. As she opened the door, a woman fell out. She was handcuffed and beaten, with a gag in her mouth. The woman had been kidnapped and raped by the two men. Kat and Grace looked at each other and told Jim and Summer to walk away, call the police, and have the manager lock the side door to the restaurant. Kat dragged the man from the floor in a choke hold to the van, and Grace told her man to sit on the ground next to his buddy.

Grace was calm, as she walked to the men on the ground, and said that she was going to slit their throats and stuff their balls in their mouths if they did not answer her questions; they have only one time to tell the truth. The men believed her and nodded their heads as Kat stood over them with her knives out. Where were you going to take the women? One of the men said to the warehouse on Fifth Ave, behind the Big Mama's Bar. Who is in charge? The men looked at each other and said that she would have them killed if they said anything else. Kat said, "I will kill you now with your balls in your mouths," as she bent over one of the men with her knife to his throat. "Wait," yelled the man; I will tell you everything; just do not kill me. It is Big Mama; she is getting paid by the cartel to supply them with women." Grace could hear the police sirens so she and Kat put away their knives. The police car pulled up to the van and they saw two women standing over two men on the ground. Jim and Summer ran to meet Kat and Grace at the side of the Waffle House. The manager explained that he had the door open to get some fresh air in order to keep his air conditioning cost down. He did not know that these men were going to harm anyone. Another patrol car pulled up; it was a patrol sergeant who asked if everything was under control and asked about the call. The responding police officer told him about the two women that foiled a kidnapping and held them down for the police to arrive. Grace and Kat saw the Lady Justice pin on his collar, and asked to speak with him. Grace smiled at the sergeant and said that they were friends with a common bond, as she pulled out a Justice Served card from her pants pocket. The sergeant asked if he could speak with them; walked off to the side, and away from the others. Grace and Kat followed as the sergeant turned to talk with them. He told his officer to take the men in and book them on attempted kidnapping and assault; more charges were to follow. The sergeant told Jim and Summer to go home; a police report will be made using the statements from Kat and Grace. Jim told the officer that he was their designated driver. The sergeant told Jim that he had it covered now and to take care of his girlfriend. Grace and Kat thanked them for a great night out and they would catch up with them later. Summer waved goodbye as Jim took her hand and walked her to his Jeep.

Now that they were alone, the sergeant wanted to know all the details. Grace filled him in on Big Mama's Bar, saying that they would take care of Big Mama and anyone else in the bar. They would pass on all the information to him. The sergeant told them that there had been multiple kidnappings from this area; mostly young good-looking women. He also wanted them to know that he would provide back-up and a cleaning crew. Grace told him that they did not need any back-up and they did not need any guns. The sergeant smiled and said, "Impressive, stay safe, and can I, at least, give you a lift?" "No thanks, but you could call us a cab?" said Grace.

Ten minutes later, a cab pulled up next to them. The driver smiled and said, "Ladies, this is on the house," and gave them his business card with a Lady Justice symbol on it. Kat looked at Grace saying, "They are everywhere, yet never seen." "Just like the ninja," said Grace. "Well said," replied Kat. The cab pulled in front of Big Ma Ma's Bar, as the driver said, "Happy hunting," as Kat and Grace got out of the cab. Grace and Kat looked at the seedy-looking place and wondered how it stayed open. As they both walked in the door, they saw a very large woman who stood behind a bar who wore a torn, white t-shirt exposing half of her large breasts with a tattoo saying Big Mama, written in black script across her chest. Her hair was black and gray pulled back; it looked dirty. Grace and Kat walked to the bar and sat next to each other. They saw a couple at a table; he was a large biker-type with a large hunting knife on his belt. The woman, sitting at the table, looked like she had been drugged; sitting there and doing nothing. She had dark rings around her eyes and her clothes looked dirty. Kat looked around the bar and saw one man who sat alone near the front door, nursing a pitcher of beer. "What can I get you two?" asked Big Mama. Grace looked at her and said, "I will have a clean glass of water." "I will have a tequila with lime and salt," replied Kat. "That's more like it; you must be the DD tonight, looking at Grace," said Big Mama. Kat turned her back on Big Mama saying, "How do you make ends meet with a place like this?" It was clearly an insult to her bar, but it went over Big Mama's head. It's getting close to closing time and most of the crowd had left the bar. She turned on the lights and yelled, "Last call for alcohol." That was the signal to the man near the front of the bar; he stood up and locked the front door, then he turned and nodded at Big Mama. Grace never got her water and Kat never got her shot of tequila with salt and lime. Big Mama looked at Grace and said, "You don't mind that I card you two cops, do you?" "Not at all," said Grace. "We aren't cops, but we are looking for a good time." Big Mama had that puzzled look on her face. The man near the front door said, "Now that's what I'm talking about."

The big biker stood up and asked, "So how do you like it?" "As rough as you can give it," said Grace. "What about you, little girl; how do you like it?" asked Big Mama. Kat smiled at her and said, "Fast and hard." "Well, I think we can help you ladies out," said Big Mama. "No, I think you have it backwards; we are the ones that are going to have fun, not you folks," replied Grace. The big biker walked up to Grace and stopped at about arm's length and pulled out his knife. "Is that all you've got?" asked Grace, as she pulled out two of her own knives from behind her back. It surprised the biker, as he took two steps back looking at Grace's knives. Big Mama leaned over the bar to try and grab Grace when Kat jumped behind the bar and saw that there was a shotgun under the bar, close to Grace. Kat yelled, "Shotgun." That made Grace move away from the bar and watch the two men that were closing in on her. "Don't hurt the merchandise, we need them," yelled, Big Mama. The biker put his knife away and grabbed a bar towel and wrapped it round his arm. Kat kicked Big Mama alongside of her left knee and heard a loud, cracking sound with Big Mama screaming in pain. The big woman was mad now and she was swinging her fists to try and hit Kat. Kat blocked all the punches, kicked her in the face, and watched her as she fell to the floor. The man from the door was getting close to Grace when Kat jumped back over the bar and stood in front of the man. The move was so fast that the man was surprised and stood still; which made him a perfect target for Kat, as she punched and kicked the man knocking him back onto the floor. The man got up saying, "Fuck this shit," as he took out his switchblade and tried to stab her in the stomach. Kat moved like a cat; she jumped out of the way of the man's wild swinging. Kat felt something was wrong and jumped up on a table top, just as a bullet went over her left ear. Kat spun around and threw her knife like a frisbee going a hundred miles an hour, hitting Big Mama in the chest; ruining her tattoo and throwing her back into the bar mirror, breaking it as she slid down to the floor. Kat now looked at the man trying to kill her and she said, "I'm going to make you eat that knife." Grace watched as the biker was not sure if he wanted to fight or run, as Grace slowly moved to cut off his escape. The biker took out his knife again and tried to stab Grace in the chest; Grace turned and grabbed his wrist, put him in a wrist lock and straightened out his arm. Grace took his knife and drove it to the hilt, as it entered his chest. Kat was now playing with the man holding the switchblade. She made him miss, as she moved easily around him, which drove him crazy with fear and anger. Kat did a jump from a table and was over the man's head when she hit the knife out of his hand with a kick. Kat held her knife at his throat, as she picked up his knife from the floor saying to him to open his mouth and say "AHH." The man opened his mouth; Kat shoved the man's knife into his mouth until only the handle was showing. Grace looked around and saw dead bodies; only the woman at the table with the biker, was still alive. She was near death, due to the drugs that were in her system. Grace called the patrol sergeant and told him of the events of their visit to Big Mama's Bar. There was a warehouse in the rear of the property that had not been searched yet, but they wanted to have the police on site before they would proceed. That sergeant thanked her and said that a cleaning crew was en-route, as was a special unit of the DEA and Homeland Security.

It was not a long wait. The police and DEA unit rolled to the rear of Big Mama's Bar, in front of the warehouse. It was big enough to hold six school buses. The police opened the doors, ready for any resistance; there was none; only the smell of filth and the moans of women in dozens of cages with buckets of waste and water near the cages, that was meant for dogs. There was a drug lab near the rear of the building, so Hazmat was called to the scene. There were six dead bodies in a pile off to the side; they had been starved to death or died from drug overdoses. The County Coroner's office was called by the patrol sergeant. He could not believe that this was happening in his city. It was so bad, that several police and DEA agents felt sick to their stomachs and had to step outside. It was sad to see so many people that had been kidnapped and used for the drug or sex trade against their will. Grace opened a large storage box and found laptops, cell phones, wallets and purses, with hundreds of loose credit cards and cash. Another tool box had watches, rings, and jewelry of every kind. Kat opened a large storage box and found hundreds of handguns and ammunition along with other large boxes marked, "Rifles, Made in China." All these items had to be counted and processed; it would be weeks before anyone could see the scope of the operation. Grace and Kat were more than ready to leave; the smell stuck to their cloths and hair. They felt dirty and wanted to go back to base for a long, hot shower or bath. The patrol sergeant called them a cab; he had been waiting, just blocks away from the scene.

The ride to Camp Yermo was quiet. The cabbie did not even try to make small talk with Grace or Kat who sat in the back seat. Grace rolled down her window, as she apologized for smelling up the cab. The cabbie just handed her a few air fresheners and asked her to hang them up anywhere, stating that he would clean the cab after shift. Kat told Grace to look on the bright side; justice had been served and they saved a lot of lives. Her only regret was that they did not save everyone. Grace had to agree with Kat, that the night was not a total waste.

As Grace looked out of the window of the cab, she thought of the young cowboy that had melted her heart and made her feel human again; listening to him sing and move with his hands, never moving from her hip or hand. Grace was ready to run away with Buck; if only he could save her from the reality that she had committed herself to, the Justice Seekers. That reality meant sacrifices for a higher purpose; the country, and the freedoms that "we the people" hold dear to our hearts. Could this country survive the crimes of the drug cartels, the human trafficking, and the theft of our resources? Grace thought about all the crime that she had seen in the last several days and it made her sick to her stomach. Then it made her mad. She screamed at the top of her lungs, out the window, which released her anger and frustration.

It startled the cabbie. He slammed on the brakes, and asked if she was alright. Kat was at her side, and understood the feelings she was going through. The cabbie started towards Camp Yermo again; it had been a long night.

The cabbie got them through the gate, without any problems, and dropped them off in front of their billet. Grace and Kat started taking their clothes off as they entered through the door. Grace said that she would bag up all the dirty cloths and put them in the dumpster as soon as possible, wishing she could just burn them instead. Kat started a shower and let the water run until it was as hot as she could handle it, without burning her skin off. Kat stood under the shower head and it felt relaxing as she let the water just hit her head. The door opened to the shower and Grace stepped in, joining Kat in the water. Nothing was said. Grace put a handful of shampoo in her hand and started to wash Kat's hair, telling her to relax. Grace washed Kat's hair, being careful not to pull or tangle her hair, saying that the smell was caused by the small molecules produced by the breakdown of the amino acids' lysine and methionine from the dead bodies, that attached to the oxygen in the air, making it stick to everything that contacted it. Kat had listened to Grace explain the medical reasons why a dead body smelled. She also noticed that Grace was gentle as she pushed her hair aside to look at her scar. Grace told Kat that she meant no disrespect by entering the shower, but explained that, in Japan, women and men bathe together. Kat turned her head and smiled saying she knew how people bathed in Japan. Grace blushed and told Kat that her Black Dragon scar was beautiful; that she knew that Kat was the Black Dragon; her grandfather was also a Black Dragon. Only a few people alive, knew the truth about Kat and it was going to stay that way. Grace and Kat finished their shower and they both stood with towels around themselves. Grace stood in front of #47 and bowed, which showed respect and she thanked her for saving her life. She would never forget the skill and discipline that she had demonstrated. #47 looked at #43 and told her that someday, she would be able to complete her training and be the next Black Dragon; she had the skills and half the training. Grace felt honored and told her that she was going to bed as she was emotionally and physically drained. #47 said that she was also going to bed and was not going to chow in the morning.

It was mid-morning when Grace woke up to the smell of tea. Kat was up watching the news out of Barstow, holding a cup of tea next to her lips. "So, what is the news saying?" asked #43. "You would not believe me, if I told you," said #47. The news woman sitting behind the desk, told the audience that the scenes they were going to show were graphic in nature. It showed several emergency people carrying body bags onto stretchers to the coroner's van and several emergency trucks with people in blankets, holding water bottles. The Department of Homeland Security stated that the DEA had raided a bar on the East side of Barstow and had confronted several people, who refused to cooperate with search warrants for the surrounding property of the bar in question. Multiple people were killed, to include the bar owner. The investigation is still ongoing but the DEA stated that a human trafficking ring and a drug lab were discovered. There were multiple victims that had been held in dog cages and were being treated. The names of the deceased have not been released, pending notification to the next of kin. Grace pointed at the television and said, "That was a load of crap; I hope someone can read between the lines. Why can't they just tell the truth?" "They are protecting us, or they were told to keep a lid on the information that was there," replied #47. Grace said that she was going to get to the bottom of it and call Mr. Jefferson. "I have an idea; let's go to lunch and think about what we are going to say; we still haven't reported to Mr. Jefferson about what really happened," said #47. "You are right. We need to get the real information out," replied Grace.

#47 was at a table in the mess hall with two bowls of rice and vegetables and a side of small pork slices. #43 joined her at the table and said that she did not see anything like that on the serving line, while she held a cheeseburger and French fries. "That is because I smiled at the staff sergeant behind the line. I remember you saying to get to know the people in the mess hall; the staff sergeant had this waiting for me. I guess he was trying to get to know me," replied #47. While they both were eating, the staff sergeant came by with some hot tea for #47 and a tall iced tea for #43 saying that if they needed anything, just ask and he will make it happen. "Thank you, staff sergeant," replied #47. "It seems that you have adjusted quite nicely to military life," said #43, smiling from ear-to-ear. As #43 and #47 finished their lunch, the command sergeant major entered the mess hall and called everyone to attention, as General Taylor entered the officer's mess hall. Everybody in the mess hall stood at attention, as he walked towards #43 and #47. He stopped in front of their table and told everyone, "At ease and enjoy your chow." #43 and #47 sat down with General Taylor, as he asked if he could join them; while he was already taking a seat. #43 looked at General Taylor and asked if this was business or pleasure? General Taylor smiled and said, "Just like you Grace, never wasting any time and getting to the point." I have good news and bad news; I will give it to you straight. I have received word from higher-up that your country needs both of you to be on a chopper, out of here at 1300 hrs today. The good news is that both of you have distinguished yourselves here with your training skills and dedication to the security of our country. The Marines of Camp Yermo are combat ready thanks to your instructions and have made the base aware of the weaknesses we have; which we are now rectifying, as we speak. We were going to have a ceremony for you and present you both with letters of appreciation and honorary titles of Marine. The bad news; I can only give you these letters and present these placards to you that tell of your extraordinary skills. You may display them on your wall at home. It is time to say good-bye; your next mission is beyond my pay grade. Good luck, Marines." The command sergeant major called, "Attention on Deck," and everyone stood at attention as General Taylor stood up.

#43 and #47 stood at attention in front of the general as he spoke in a loud commanding voice. "Today we honor two civilian contractors that came to Camp Yermo to better prepare us for combat. They have shown us what discipline and dedication are,

through the Marine's motto, "Adapt, Improvise and Overcome". Their shooting skills are that of a range master, which is a testament to their training skills. The Commandant of the Marines has deemed them as honorary Marines in title, as Warrant Officer Combative Instructors." The general held out his hand to congratulate them. As he shook their hands, he put a challenge coin in their hands. #43 stood at attention and felt overwhelmed with so many emotions, that tears rolled down her face. #43 felt the pride and honor that all Marines held with the title of Marine. #47 looked down at the coin in her hand and bowed. She returned the favor by taking the general's hand and giving him a throwing star with the Iga symbol in the center. The general had never received a coin from a lesser rank before; now he felt honored at the gift he received and said, "Semper Fi ,Marine." #47 gave a "OOHRAH," at the top of her lungs.

13

JUST A TOURIST

BY THE TIME #43 and #47 returned to their billet, after shaking hands with everyone at the mess hall, they only had forty-minutes to pack and be at the landing zone in front of headquarters. There were a lot of questions that they were going over, out loud. #47 asked if they were now part of the military? #43 told her it was, in title only, so do not worry. "Who is sending us on a mission that the general does not even know about? Who is higher up than him?" asked #47. #43 told her to slow down; something must have happened. I will bet that Mr. Jefferson has something to do with all of this." Both of their phones went off at the same time. It was Mr. Jefferson. "Sorry if I interrupted your party, but an incident has occurred that needs your immediate attention. You will take a short flight to Camp Pendleton, where you will be taken to a secure location. I will meet you there for the briefing."

#43 and #47 knew that Mr. Jefferson would not tell them anything until he saw them; so they did not bother to ask him. They were packed and their ride was waiting. As they exited their billet, nearly all the camp had formed a line on both sides of the road. All the troops gave a "OOHRAH." and started to sing the Marine Corps Hymn. It was an amazing display of honor given to the instructors; as honorary Marines for Camp Yermo; they would not be forgotten anytime soon. The Humvee pulled up to the landing pad and Sergeant James Thomas was waiting. "I thought you had the weekend off?" said #43. "With all due respect, I couldn't let you both leave without saying how honored I am to have been trained by the best; thank you for everything," replied Sergeant James Thomas, with a salute, a handshake and gave them both a Camp Yermo challenge coin.

Out of nowhere, a US Marine Osprey seem to fall out of the sky, landed and waited for the two instructors to board. Without delay, the plane took off vertically and headed towards San Diego. #43 and #47 put on the head-set and listened to what the pilot had to say about the trip. #43 looked down at her hand and saw that her coin had a small note taped to the back of it. #43 smiled and took the tape off and read the note.

> *"Dear Grace, I must confess I was smitten by you, waiting ten years seems like a lifetime but it would be worth it. Here is my number if you decide to change your mind on a shorter wait period. Forever yours, Buck."*

#47 saw tears on #43's face as she smiled and put her note and coin inside of her bra, next to her heart. #43 looked at #47 and said, "I think this will be my last mission. I have a date with destiny. My heart says to follow my gut." #47 smiled and asked, "Sure you are not just hungry?"

Time went by fast as they both looked out of the small windows. The pilot came over the headset said it would be thirty-five minutes to touch down. #43 told #47 she was nervous about the mission, but she did not know why. #47 told her it was because she had a reason to be careful and that the note next to her heart had a lot to do with being nervous. #43 agreed; she had to get her head in the game fast, or death would be her destiny.

The Marine Osprey made its landing without any fanfare. #43 and #47 left the plane carrying their bags to a waiting, black GMC suv. The ride was short as the GMC drove into a hanger with two people closing the doors. The GMC came to a stop in front of a desk. Mr. Jefferson stood next to the desk with a worried look on his face, as he held out his hand to welcome #43 and #47. "Let's cut to the chase; what is going on?" asked #43. "You look terrible," said #43. Mr. Jefferson explained, "We have a huge problem, and we only have sixteen hours left to fix it. Two senators have had their daughters kidnapped from a beach in Tijuana, Mexico. They were there to do some shopping while on Spring Break, and the Cartel got wind of their visit. They are demanding ten-million-dollars and say that they will send them back in pieces if the police or military get involved. They sent a proof of life video to the American Embassy. The girls' chaperons were killed, along with two other students that got in the way. The Mexican Government said it was collateral damage. We know who is running that place, so there is no need to ask. They are not going to help us. The girls are being held at a hotel near the beach, and the local police have been bought by the Cartel. We are between a rock and a hard place. I want you both to know, up front, that these two senators are close friends of mine and we exchange favors from time to time.

They came to me first. If word gets out to the media about this, they will be removed from their committees, as being compromised. This is a private matter and the military cannot be used, as it would look like an unauthorized action on foreign soil. We all know that the cartels have control of the border, and we know that there are some border patrol officers on their payroll. I have access to all the maps and material support; it is people that I can trust with my life that are hard to find. The Justice Seekers that I have on hand are not ready to be in the field. I need more time that I do not have; I am asking you, #47 and you, #43 to take this mission, knowing that it could be a one-way ticket. I have no one else; I am begging you," said Mr. Jefferson.

#43 and #47 looked at each other and gave a nod. "We will get the girls and bring them home if we can," said #43. "This is not a Justice Seeker mission for the books. This will be to honor our friendship and trust," replied #47. "Tell me what you need," replied Mr. Jefferson. #43 took lead on this operation and requested up-to-date thermal imaging on the hotel and photos of the two girls with any medical information. #47 said she would make a list of needed items, to include weapons of choice. An hour had passed and Mr. Jefferson was still making phone calls to make things happen. The hard part was waiting for it to be dark. The plan was to drop in by hang glider; an extraction by air, on the beach near the hotel. It would be a night for a ninja, with #43 being her cover. #47 would be wearing her classic black ninja uniform with added protection. All her weapons were silent; the bow, sword, darts, the knives and her skills. #47 and #43 would be carrying two harnesses and one-hundred-feet of black rope for the extraction of the two girls. #43 would also wear all black clothing, but she would have two Sig Sauer's P-226 in 40 caliber with suppressors and have six extra magazines around her waist, with her two long knives in her boots. There were no friendlies and no outside help. The only thing they had on their side, was surprise. The cartel had men inside and outside of the hotel,l with a roving patrol along the beach. The odds were not good and they could be walking into a trap. They had all the information they needed; now it was up to the good Lord and their skills. #43 and #47 reviewed the area where they were to land and told Mr. Jefferson that they would do their best. Mr. Jefferson knew the risk and told them just to make it back, and do what they do best. An AC-130 was waiting to take a thirty-minute hop, just over the border and return home; minus two female warriors dressed in black. The clock was ticking; the girls would be fish-food at six o'clock if the demands were not met.

Flying silently, the two black warriors saw the landmarks where they needed to glide into the landing zone. There was very little traffic and there was no full moon. So far, luck was on their side, as they slid to the ground without any problems. #43 and #47 put in their ear wigs for communication and folded up the hang gliders. It was only two-hundred yards to the hotel and they were making good time staying in the shadows and off the road. A jeep, with four men carrying automatic rifles, drove passed them heading towards the hotel; it was a roving patrol. Mr. Jefferson gave them an update on the two girls; thermal imaging showed two bodies in the same location for the pass four hours. They were in a small room, on the right-hand side of the main lobby; probably a restroom or closet.

"Copy," replied #43. #47 told #43 that she wanted the high ground, and #43 gave her a nod in agreement. They scaled a two-story warehouse across from the hotel; it was a good choice, as they had the advantage and nobody had seen them. There were four men on the roof of the hotel smoking and looking out at the ocean. #47 took out her bow and #43 held her hand and pointed to her gun. It was risky to make four head shots at fifty yards, but the odds were in her favor as none of the men held their rifles or had pistols. #47 gave a nod and put an arrow in her bow as back up. The men started to move around and reach for their rifles. They never had a chance to touch them, as they each received a bullet to the head, without making a sound and fell. #47 attached a small claw to the end of the rope and threw the rope across to the roof. This was not her first rodeo; she tied the end to a pole that held a satellite and went across upside down as if it were nothing. #43 smiled, remembering the training with the Marines. #43 followed and checked the dead bodies for a radio. There was none; that meant that other men would come to relieve them. The question was when.

#47 grabbed her rope and took her claw and put it away. She took the rope and threw it to the other side. #43 gave a sitrep (military for "situational report"), to Mr. Jefferson; that they were still on the hunt to find the girls. #47 looked over the hotel, down into the street, and saw the jeep going by again. She counted eight men in the front and two standing near the back employee entrance. #47 told #43 that she would take out the two at the employee entrance and get to the girls. It was up to #43 to take out anyone from the front of the hotel. #43 nodded and told her, "Happy hunting." #47 smiled and disappeared into the dark. The two men at the employee entrance were smoking and talking when a shadow went by them and startled them. They each looked at each other, as blood flowed from their necks, and fell to the ground with their eyes wide open in disbelief. #47 went over the coms saying, "In and hunting." #47 went into the hotel and up some stairs to the main floor. She heard some voices, but they went away from her, towards the lobby. #43 was at the corner of the hotel watching the front when the jeep came around the corner. #43 hid in some bushes and waited for the jeep to pass; but luck was not with her, as the jeep stopped at the corner and the men got out. The men were only a few feet away when #43 stepped out into the open holding her Sig just feet away from the driver's head. #43 pulled the trigger spraying brain matter on one of the men. #43 pulled the trigger three more times before anyone could get off a shot or sound an alarm. #43 checked them for radios; nobody had radios, just weapons and cell phones. #43 picked up the bodies and put them into the jeep with their chins resting on their chests. They were out of play for good. #43 spoke into her comm stating that the jeep patrol was out of play, at the corner of the hotel. "Roger that," in reply.

#47 asked for an update on any heat signatures in the lobby area. "None," came the reply. Mr. Jefferson had to work some of his magic and fast. Bodies were falling and nobody was making any calls to check in. #47 caught a break when she heard some crying from a closet and opened the door to find two young girls tied up with duct tape at the wrists and feet with a rag covering their mouths. #47 must have scared them half to death, being dressed in black with knives out. That changed when #47 cut the tape from both girls and told them to be very quiet, if they wanted to live, and to follow her. The girls nodded their heads and said that the cartel took two of their friends to the pool area. #47 asked them their names. They were indeed the senators' daughters; they were the package that had to be returned unharmed. #47 sent out the good news over the comm and said that she was heading to the beach for pickup. #43 replied that she would provide cover and try to find the other two girls near the pool.

The order was given to send in the Osprey for pick up. It would be a long thirty minutes before pickup and there were still a lot of bad men in the area. #43 heard the loud laughing from the men that were raping the young girls at the side of the pool. The girls were scream-ing, as they were being hit and raped; the men stood around; were half naked and drinking, while they waited their turn with the girls. It seemed that everyone was having a good time until one of the men saw two girls running towards the ocean. Three of the men started to run after them, in just their underwear; which was unfair, seeing that they had no weapons. #47 waited until the men reached her before she stood up from the sand, and killed them without any remorse. The girls were still running to the water's edge when someone started to shoot at them. #43 saw that there were two men shooting at them from the balcony. That was short-lived. #43 got their attention when she yelled at them to look down. The men looked down at her, which made great targets for her. She put two rounds into their heads and went to the pool where she heard men yelling at each other. There were four men half-dressed, and two who were putting on their boots. Their rifles were leaning on the wall near them. The girls were on the ground crying and curled up in a ball. #43 ran towards the men with both guns in her hands; the men were stunned to see that a woman was challeng-ing them. #43 pointed her guns and killed six men on the run. They received multiple gun shots to their chests and heads. #43 was near the girls and told them to run to the ocean, if they wanted to get back home. The girls looked up at #43 and started to run towards the ocean.

#43 reloaded her guns and stood her ground near the pool ,making sure that everyone had a chance to be saved. #47 had the girls kneeling in a group near the water's edge to make them a smaller target. It was dark near the water, and sound carried over the sandy beach. #43 heard men yelling and running towards the pool. #43 took a knee by the wall of the pool, and waited for the men to appear, while she looked to see what other weapons the dead men left behind. There were two AK47's and one deer rifle with a scope. #43 kept a mental note of how much ammo she had left and available near her; she hoped that the Calvary would arrive soon, as it would be daylight soon and everyone would be a sitting duck.

#43 did not have to wait long; several men ran into the pool area and looked for the girls and instead, saw several of their men dead. They yelled in Spanish at each other, saying that they would be thrown into the wood chipper by the boss if they did not find the girls. Before the men split up, #43 slowly stood up and took aim at two of the men and shot them in the head. This startled the others as they turned towards #43, who had already had them in her sights. She squeezed the trigger, making every round count, and hit her targets. One man was lucky, as he jumped over the wall and ran like he was on fire around the corner of the building. #43 picked up an AK47 and ran towards the ocean in a zig- zag fashion; crouched down, she was became invisible to the naked eye. #43 met with #47 and the other girls who were shivering with cold due to the lack of clothes and the ocean water in which they were standing. #47 and #43 both heard a truck driving on the beach, with the headlights on high-beams and some spotlights used for off-road driving. This was not a good sign. #43 said that she had it covered, and to keep the girls safe. #43 ran off towards the truck and dodged the lights. #47 told the girls to move farther down the beach, away from the truck and to stay with each other. #47 put herself between the truck and the girls. The truck was getting closer, when #43 got into range with the AK47 and shot at the lights and the driver's side door. Everything was dark again, with some gun fire coming from the truck. #47 watched as she saw gun fire from #43, unload everything she had, until there was nobody shooting back.

#47 felt the wind first and then the sound of the Osprey coming down out of the black sky. It landed only ten yards from where the girls were standing. The rear ramp was down and there were two Marines holding rifles with night scopes on them. The girls ran into the plane and #47 was right behind them, looking into the darkness for #43. The Marines yelled that they had to leave now. #47 told them, "Over my dead body," as she put a knife to the throat of a Marine saying that she would leave not leave anyone behind. #43 came running to the ramp and jumped, just as the Osprey was lifting off. As the ramp was rising, #43 was knocked back off her feet. She had been shot in the chest; a small, blood ring appeared. #47 screamed at the top of her lungs, and ran to #43 and held her. One of the Marines took off his helmet and grabbed a first aid kit and told the pilot that they had one down in the back. The pilot's radio transmission was short; "One down and the package was safe with two others. Emergency personnel to report to the landing twenty-five minutes out. #47 was still holding #43 with tears running down her face, yelling at her to live. The Marine was taking #43's vitals when he looked at #47 saying he had a pulse. #47 ripped open the shirt of #43 and saw that the challenge coin had been hit, with the bullet still in the coin. The bleeding was minimal, but it had knocked #43 out, due to the force of the bullet hitting her square in the chest with the coin stopping the bullet. #43 was unconscious, but alive. #47 was madder than hell. They should have had bullet-proof vests; they were not expendables. The girls came over to see #43 lying in #47's lap. They talked about her bravery and her skills; they were glad that she was alive. They told #47 about their ordeal with the Mexican Cartel and how they raped and murdered their chaperons by throwing them into a wood chipper and laughing about it. They had seen the worst of criminals and the best of others who lay down their lives in order to save a few girls who went shopping on Spring Break in Mexico. Life would never be the same for them, and they would tell their story to others who would think of traveling abroad to party and find new adventures in another country. #47 hated the Cartels as much as the Yakuza or Triads; they were all the worst mankind had to offer, and they showed no mercy.

A few minutes to touch down; #43 was moaning in pain and awake. #47 told her not to move around until she had been checked out by the medical team on standby at the landing zone. The girls had blankets around them when they were met by the medical teams who took them to a secure location. #43 was last out of the Osprey, to be seen by the medics, with #47 by her side. Mr. Jefferson was also waiting with the medical teams and saw #47 giving him a dirty look. The Marine that had helped #43 asked #47 if she really would have killed him? #47 looked at him and he knew he should not have asked the question. He said that he was sorry that #43 had been shot.

The medical team told Mr. Jefferson that they were witnesses to a miracle. They had never seen a bullet in a challenge coin; it had saved #43's life. #43 would have a large bruise in the center of her chest and the bullet wound would heal. It had only broken the skin, with very minimal damage. Mr. Jefferson told them he was very grateful for their service. #47 had been listening the whole time and waited for the right opportunity to talk to Mr. Jefferson alone. The mission was a success, but it still cost the lives of two innocent people. The odds were against them from the start, and the Mexican government or the Federal Police did nothing to help the U.S. Senators; the odds were stacked against them. It was clear that the cartels ran the cities and half of the government was corrupt.

#47 saw Mr. Jefferson talking on the phone. He did not sound happy with the other person on the phone. When he was done talking, he went to #47 and asked for a few minutes alone. #47 walked ahead of

Mr. Jefferson, out of the building and turned around to face him. She was visibly upset and had a lot to say to Mr. Jefferson. Mr. Jefferson stood in front of her to hear what the little warrior had to say, and he knew it was not going to be a nice conversation. He looked at #47 and said, "I am responsible for what transpired; it could have been worse, but I did my best in the short time I had to put the mission together. What could I have done better? I do not want to make the same mistake again with the members of the Justice Seekers." #47 looked him in the eyes, and told him, "Know your enemy, have better resources to protect your people, and do not trust the government. Our enemy is in all parts of the system that we call our government, and lastly, do not let your heart over-rule your head. Trust your people."

The Senator's daughters were raped and nearly killed, but they were able to get valuable information. They heard that there are several tunnels that run directly into San Diego that are being used for drug and human trafficking. There are many CEO's and influential people that are on the cartel's payroll. They are in our city's corporations, banking institutions and government. They heard that their kidnapping was in retaliation for not easing restrictions on the border. If any of this is true, the Justice Seekers must be deployed to stop and uncover the truth.

Mr. Jefferson lowered his head and said, "#47, you are correct; everything you have said, is true. My problem is that some of my best assets are not ready to deploy; you have been the first to not go through training because of your deadly skills and natural abilities. You are a proven warrior; you think outside of the box, and have great instincts. #43 (Grace) has filled me in on every aspect of your training. I know she meant well by watching over you, and you have a close relationship with her after working together on so many projects. I could not be prouder of the way you have conducted yourself in the field."

It was two days before #43 was released from the hospital, and she was happy to be walking on her own. #43 had done a lot of soul-searching, after nearly being killed. She had a small reminder just how human she was and fortunate that she could tell her story. #47 had not left her side during the whole time she was in the hospital, except for about forty-five minutes. She needed a change of clothes and she had something special to put on that nasty bruise that #43 had in the middle of her chest. #43 did not mind the smell and it did the trick. The doctors and nurses thought it was a medical miracle; the healing was several times faster than expected. Mr. Jefferson was waiting to see her to see if she would be willing to give him a verbal report on the events that had happened at the beach hotel. #43 gave him the short version and said she did not remember much after getting shot. #43 smiled at #47 and thanked her for being there with her the entire time, and told her she was the best partner one could ever ask for in any lifetime. #43 took out a white envelope and handed it to Mr. Jefferson with a smile, saying, "This is my destiny and I would like the Justice Council to release me of my oath as Justice Seeker. I have a young man waiting for me and I am not going to pass this up. I am not sure where it is going to lead me, but one thing is for sure, I will not be dodging bullets." #43 looked at #47 and asked her to be her bride's maid when the time comes, and asked Mr. Jefferson if he would do the honor of walking her down the aisle. Mr. Jefferson looked happy, and sad at the same time, and said, "Of course. I have lost a warrior and gained a daughter. I will make sure this gets the approval without any problems." He held up her envelope and walked away.

#43 took #47's hand and held it, saying that the best was yet to come for her; she had to follow her own path and listen to her feelings and gut instinct. This was the right decision for #43. She has a chance to start a new life without blood and bullets; but knew that she would always be looking over her shoulder. #47 told #43 that it was an honor to have had her as a partner and trainer; "Always ready Never surprised." #43 replied, "We will meet again in this life or the next, and I will be ready."

"So, what would you say about coming with me to a certain bar that has dancing and music and serves tequila?" asked #43. #47 smiled and said, "You do not have to ask me twice. Are we looking for a young man named Buck?" #43 laughed and said, "That's what is on my mind; we need some R & R."

14

TROUBLE IN PARADISE

#43 MADE A call to Mr. Jefferson and told him about their trip for some much needed R & R. The conversation was short and had his blessing. He told her it was a well-deserved time off, but if they needed anything, all she had to do is ask. "We need to call Sergeant Thomas and give him a heads up; we are a few days out. I would like to buy some real clothes and get some rest before the road trip," said #47. #43 agreed, and said she needed to rest up, so they found a nice hotel to recharge themselves. Their stay was just OK; they would have liked to have been sleeping in until nine o'clock. That would have been priceless. They made it down to the lobby where breakfast was still being served and the last of the hot items were just put out. #47 asked if it was OK to take food with them? "Sure, just do not empty the pans in your bag." #43 laughed and asked if she was talking to her inner feelings or her stomach. #47 smiled and said, "My stomach," as she was making her second waffle. #43 looked at the bruise on her chest, and saw that it was healing just fine, and hoped that it would be gone within the next few days. Sitting at the table with #47 was always fun to watch, as she was known to eat like it was her last meal. #43 had a box of OJ, a banana and some yogurt. #47 asked if she felt alright, because she did not have to eat like she was still in the hospital. #43 laughed, and said that she was eating enough for both of them.

The drive to Barstow was long and they both wanted to eat and sleep in a nice, comfortable bed. #43 will call Sergeant Thomas in the morning, and tell him they were in town for several days on R & R. #47 asked #43 if she had made any plans about her future with Buck. #43 told her that she was still thinking about how to tell Buck that she was now available. #43 also said that she wanted to check on Buck to see what he was all about; she did not want any surprises or a wife hunting her down with kids in tow. "Maybe, you should date him for a bit; you do not want to be his sugar mama," said #47. "True, maybe I will get a small apartment with a six-month lease and see how things pan out," said #43. #47 reminded her that once she walks away, that is it; no more #43. "I am good with walking away; nothing will ever change my mind about that. All I must do is look at my challenge coin as a wake-up call. Life is too short," replied #43. "Yes, it is," replied #47.

They both found a place to stay until they felt ready to hit the town. It was over dinner one evening when #47 asked #43 if she would like to be alone for a few days while she checked on a few things before she left the fold. #43 said that she would be OK, but would miss her company. #43 smiled, and asked if she was going to look for trouble? #47 told her that trouble always was able to find her; that was the problem. "If you want some back-up, you know where to find me," said #43. "I will try to be a good girl, but I think I can handle myself," said #47, as she got up to find the lady's room. As #47 walked away, #43 realized that her partner was trying to prepare her for a different life, outside of the Justice Seekers, and that did not sit well with her at first. #43 pulled the coin out from the side of her bra; the bullet was still seated in the center of the coin. She wanted some payback and, at the same time, she wanted to be in love and hold onto Buck while she was still alive.

That night at the hotel, #47 told #43 that she was going out and not to wait up for her; she would be back in the morning. #43 smiled and told her, "That if she couldn't be good, be the best at whatever you do." #47 smiled and told her," Always ready Never surprised." Once in the lobby, #43 called Sergeant Thomas to see if he could pick her up. Sergeant Thomas was more than happy to meet her. He asked about Grace. Buck had been asking him every other day, if he had heard anything from her. Sergeant Thomas told him the truth; he did not know anything, but was able to get the coin to her as she was leaving. Sergeant Thomas said that Buck told him that he, "Got it bad; the love bug bit him to the bone bad, and all he could think about was Grace." Sergeant Thomas said that he did not think that he even danced with another woman since he walked Grace off the dance floor. #47 told Sergeant Thomas that Grace felt the same way and was thinking about staying in the area just for Buck. Sergeant Thomas said, "Who would have guessed that those two would hit it off after just one dance. I will be there to pick you up in thirty. I'm already on the road, see ya soon, Kat."

#47 sat in the lobby, waiting and watching people as they walked into and out of the lobby. Most of them were couples; travelers from out of state. #47 smiled as she heard Sergeant Thomas, aka Jim, pull up to the doors. Summer came into the lobby, hugged her and told her that she missed them. Summer asked if Grace was coming? "Not this time," replied Kat. "It is too bad Buck is lonely and love sick. He sucks on one beer all night and is always watching the door to see if Grace is coming in. We need to get them together soon, if you know what I mean," as she giggled and grabbed Jim by the arm. "Where to?" asked Jim, looking at Kat. She said, "Let's find Buck; we need to talk." Summer was nonstop with the laughing and match-making talk. Jim was just smiling and listening and watched as Kat's eyes had that glazed-over look. Summer was just a ball of energy and excited to hear that Grace was back in town. Jim pulled up in the parking lot of the bar to see a small crowd. Several men were fighting and Buck was in the center of the men, hitting and being hit; he gave it as well as he got it. Jim called Buck, but he did not look; he was punching, kicking, and still fighting. Kat looked around and walked into the crowd of men. One of the men grabbed her arm and he went flying to the ground. Kat now had several of the men's attention, as she walked up to Buck. Buck saw her and stopped throwing punches. One of the men thought it was a good idea to hit Buck when he was not looking. That was a bad idea. Kat caught the fist in her hand and pulled him off balance toward her. The moves that followed, were too fast to watch as the man yelled and screamed for mercy as his arm was dislocated. The men scattered and left the area, leaving Buck standing with a bloody lip and a small cut above his left eye. If there had been any Marines there, they would have run the other way; everybody knew Sensi Katsumi was a hand-to-hand combat instructor. The first words out of Buck's mouth were, "Is Grace with you?" "Yes, but we have to talk first; let us get you cleaned up." "Is she OK? What happened? Why isn't she here?" Buck kept up with the twenty questions until Kat grabbed his face and told him to look into her eyes; she meant business and told him to sit down while Summer got some water and Jim got a rag to clean his face. Buck was upset and just looked down at the ground knowing that something bad had happened; he had a sick feeling in his stomach. Kat had everybody sit down while she explained that they had been doing a private security job and Grace was shot in the chest. Buck started to cry. "Grace is alive and well; the coin saved her life and your note gave her hope and the will to live for something better. I am here to ask you if you had made any plans for your future; her future with you? Life is not a fairy tale of running off into the sunset happily ever after," said Kat. "I know that," said Buck.

My dad and uncle just sold our ranch that had been in our family for generations. We loved that place, but he would not say why he sold it. We got a fair market value, but we do not have a place to call home anymore. I do the rodeo circuit, which keeps me on the road nine months of the year traveling, but I get jobs working on big ranches, if I'm willing to work there. I am pretty sure that I could settle down in one place with the right job. My head is spinning with Grace on my mind; I never felt this way before about a woman. I told my dad and uncle about Grace and they said to keep things simple, be honest, and always tell her how you feel. My dad says to hold on tight, but let her have her space. "Your dad is a wise man," replied Kat. "I have some savings put aside for those rainy days; my mom would say do not wait until the well is dry to get a drink of water." "I am here to help you plan with Grace; she is willing to quit her security job for you. Being stuck in a home, even with you, is not fair to her. I am her friend and she saved my life. I am looking out for you both. Remember that life is short and to follow your path of happiness," said Kat.

Jim asked Buck if he could give more details of the sale of their ranch. He had heard that several ranches around the area had been sold under the radar, so to speak, to some Chinese corporation. Kat looked at Jim and asked if they can do that? Can a foreign country buy land of another country? "Only in America," said Summer. Kat remembered the incident in Pueblo; China has their hands in everything that America owns or builds; stores, banks, tech information and politicians. "I think I will have to look into this further," said Kat. Summer asked if everybody was good. She wanted to go inside to dance and have a few drinks. Jim smiled and told her to lead the way. Kat held her hand out for Buck, to help him get up. He noticed how strong she was for her size, and her grip was crushing his hand as she pulled him up. "Would you ever consider bull riding? Your grip is incredible," said Buck. "I'll keep that in mind," said Kat, as they walked toward the bar.

The group was within feet of the door when a voice asked Buck if he was up to a dance? Buck turned to see that Grace was right behind him. Before another word was said, Buck and Grace were locked arm and body, holding and kissing each other as if nobody was around. Kat smiled and Jim and Summer held each other and watched as the two lovers still were in a deep moment between themselves. Grace started to say that she had been wanting to tell him what she did, but Buck just keep kissing and holding her. "Does this mean you will stay?" asked Buck. Grace kissed him saying, "Yes, I'll be staying as long as you will have me." Buck turned and looked at everybody, and then looked at Grace in the eyes and said, "I have a plan. Will you marry me?" Buck got down on one knee and dug out a ring from his front pocket; it was a big, beautiful diamond. Grace started to cry and said, "Yes, if you will promise to make all my dreams come true." "I will die trying to keep our dreams alive, with all of my heart. I will do my very best," replied Buck.

The doors to the bar were open and everybody there watched as Buck asked for Grace's hand. There was not a dry eye in the place and the group never bought a drink that night. The manager told Buck that the place was his whatever day he wanted to have his wedding reception, and there would be an open bar.

Kat stood at the bar with Jim and Summer and said, "I did not see that one coming. He had a plan all along, and never said a word." Grace and Buck were on the dance floor and never walked off to have a drink. The music could have stopped and they still would be out there dancing. Jim told Kat and Summer that someone was going to have to say something to the love birds; it was getting close to closing time and he had to go to work in the morning. Kat walked up to Grace and Buck and told them that it was time to go. Grace looked at Kat and told her to go back to the hotel; they were going to find other sleeping arrangements nearby, and not to worry or wait up. Kat did not see that one coming either, as she walked up to Jim and Summer and asked Jim for a ride back to the hotel. "No problem," said Jim. "I need to make a pit-stop before we hit the road." Summer gave Jim a kiss goodnight and said he owes her one. Kat turned to say goodbye to Grace and Buck, but she was too late; they had vanished into the night.

The ride to the hotel was quiet. Jim was talking, but Kat did not hear a word he said. Kat was thinking hard about Grace and Buck; she wanted the best for them and she realized that she had gotten too close to Grace and had forgotten some of her Iga training. Kat wanted to find out more information about the China land grab and the Mexican drug cartel's reach. Why was the truth not told by the news? Why were the police or Border Patrol looking the other way instead of into the drug and human trafficking? Kat wanted to end her R & R; it was time to get back to work. She may have lost her partner, but she still had a reminder on her back. She had a mission to complete for her family. Kat went to bed restless and was not able to sleep more than a few minutes at a time. After a few hours, she just got up and dressed. She started to make some tea and do some meditation to get her mind to focus. Kat sat outside, and watched as the sun started to rise; it was one of the most beautiful sights at five-thirty in the morning.

At seven-thirty, Kat was sitting on the floor at her coffee table in her hotel room having another cup of tea, when the phone rang; it was Mr. Jefferson. Kat had been thinking about calling him and it happened. They talked for over an hour. They talked about Grace, their past missions, and the things that still needed to be done. Kat learned of a new team out of Colorado. #38 were a married couple and were just finishing up with some last-minute training; they sounded very promising. Mr. Jefferson said that their paths would meet in the not-too-distant future. He asked #47 to hold off on several of her requests due to the mission status of #38. #47 did get the OK to find out more information about the drug cartels and human trafficking going on in Nevada and Arizona. #47 was given some leads for follow-up, and an SUV would be sent to her location with all the things needed for a recon mission. Kat was excited that she was on her own now, and that she had a recon mission; no distractions, and no surprises. #47 packed her backpack with everything a ninja would need to be invisible. She could not afford to make any mistakes. She was alone on this mission, and she needed to get the information needed, to Mr. Jefferson.

#47 sat on the coffee table with her legs crossed; it was the perfect height to look out the window into the parking lot. Twenty-five minutes had passed when she saw a dark blue SUV pull up just outside her door. #47 watched as the driver did not look around; he just walked straight up to the door and knocked. #47 opened the door and saw a young man with a Lady Justice pin on his collar. The young man told her that if there was anything else that she needed, to please call, without hesitation. #47 took the small envelope and handed him a tip. The young man turned down the tip and told her that it was a kind gesture, but he would rather see justice done and walked away.

#47 drove south on I-15 to San Diego, where she would rest up after a long drive. #47 thought about all the equipment that was in the SUV; it was worth thousands of dollars. Mr. Jefferson was sparing no expense; he had listened to her; Justice Seekers are not expendable. It was at this moment, that #47 had an idea to enter Mexico at night, by using her skills as a ninja, to find a way into the heart of cartel territory. #47 drove around looking at the border signs; looking for a way into Mexico undetected. She found a fence where some locals were walking. Several trails led into, and out of Mexico. There were no customs agents or police watching these areas. After a few minutes, #47 saw signs that read, "Cameras in Use". A few cameras were mounted under the bridge and a few on some light poles. They could be watched, but they were not stopped; that did not make any sense to her. #47 found a suitable place to park her SUV, and watched the locals come and go.

It was late that night, when #47 had repacked her backpack and checked her equipment for her journey into Mexico. #47 called Mr.

Jefferson to advise him that she was going dark and to pick up the SUV. It would be several days before she would make contact again. Mr. Jefferson was nervous about her mission, but knew that if anyone could it, she would be the one to do it. He told her to input several numbers to memory. She could use any phone, and it would bring help to her, no matter the location. His last words were ,"God's speed and come home."

15

PANDORA'S BOX

#47 WALKED SOUTH, and followed the trail that had been made by so many others before. She kept her head down, with her black hood covering half of her face. She had walked about two miles, when she realized that there was no more foot traffic behind her or in front of her. The trail had her close to the highway, and she could be seen by any vehicle's headlights. #47 felt it was not the time to get stopped by anyone, so she walked down from the trail, out of sight from any lights. A large covered truck stopped alongside the road and several men got out with large spot lights, which lit up the trail for a hundred yards. #47 quickly hid in the tall grass, making use of all the shadows. The men were shouting in Spanish. They were looking for someone; it could not have been her, as she had been very careful not to be seen. #47 heard voices of females, who were crying and screaming, but could not help them without being compromised.

Hector Jesus Ramos adjusted his hat to cover his eyes so the females could not see his anger. He grabbed a female from the truck by her hair and dragged her to the edge of the road. He forced her to look out into the darkness, as he used his spot light. He yelled in her face and forced her to close her eyes; his smell and breath made her want to vomit. Hector yelled into the truck at the remaining women, as they watched as their fellow prisoner was being held by the hair. Hector showed no feelings towards the woman, as he pulled out his gun and held it to the woman's head. There was a moment of silence, as the woman made the sign of the cross. Hector pulled the trigger, without hesitation, and pushed her down the embankment. The body slid by #47. The woman was in her early twenties. #47 saw an opportunity to hitch a ride, as the men got back into the truck. Luck was on her side. All of the men got back into the cab. Just as the driver started the truck, his door swung open. A short sword entered into his neck. He died, holding his throat, thinking that he could stop the bleeding. Men from the crew cab started to yell at each other and tried to pull out their guns; it was of no use. #47 had them at a disadvantage and they could not move. #47 looked at the terrified man as he saw a blade entering his chest cavity; it was the same with the other two men who were stuck in the small cab area. Hector was sitting in the passenger seat across from the driver when he saw his driver killed.

He was thinking on his feet, and got out of the cab while his men were being killed. Hector pulled out his pistol and waved his gun, while he yelled at a dark figure; he felt a slight breeze pass by him as he felt a burning feeling from his right hand, as it hit the ground. Hector was in shock to see his hand holding a gun on the ground. He grabbed his bloody stump, and yelled at the dark figure. #47 stood next to him and held her sword at his neck. This scared Hector and called her a witch from hell. "Speak English?" asked #47. "Yes, you fucking witch," replied Hector. "Good, stay here and don't move, or I will cut off your legs," replied #47. #47 went to the back of the truck and told the women that they were free and to use the trail going North. The women hurried out of the truck and started to go down the embankment. One woman stayed behind to tell the dark figure that Hector was from the Complex; he was a very bad and dangerous man. #47 just gave her a nod and pointed her North. #47 walked back to Hector and looked at the bloody stump saying, "You will live, if you don't lose any more blood." Hector was pale and sweating; still holding his wrist with his hand. "Hector, we are going to have a little conversation, and you will tell me every-thing or you might not make it out of here alive," said #47.

The interrogation went very well for the first hour; after that, Hector started to go in and out of consciousness, making up things and calling her names in Spanish. He was taking too long to give her correct, simple answers to easy questions, so she cut him on the arm and face. Her last question was, "Where is the Complex?" Hector just smiled and said, "Fly to hell you witch." "You go there first,"said #47, and with a single move, removed his head from his body. He was no longer a dangerous man, as his head rolled down the same embank-ment as the young woman he had shot.

#47 now went through the truck, pulled out the dead bodies, and rolled them down the embankment with Hector. She found a half-bloody towel in the cab and wiped a spot so she could drive the truck far enough away from the dead bodies to not draw any attention. The road was dark with few signs. She saw a large, lighted area to the right, with an airstrip. A sign saying, "The Complex", was too good to be true, but it had to be; it was the only thing out in the middle of nowhere. #47 drove the truck within a half mile of The Complex, before she drove it into a ravine, where nobody would spot it. #47 knew she would never be that lucky, but she could always hope.

Jogging to the fence line of The Complex was easy, but trying to go unnoticed would be another thing. The place was lit up and there were no shadows to hid in, or run into. As luck would have it, there was a vehicle and walking patrols all over the place. #47 started to slowly walk the fence line looking for a weakness; it came down to the airstrip itself. She was going to have to walk, or crawl, her way into the Complex, before the sun came up, which would be soon. #47 walked a few feet from the fence, when she saw a drainage pipe that went under the fence to the middle of the runway; it was used to keep water from standing on the runway.

#47 wasted no time and entered the drain pipe and crawled her way into the Complex. If she had a bigger frame, she would never have fit. To get through, she had to take off her backpack and pull it behind her. The pipe ran down the middle of the runway for another two-hundred yards, with drainage grates every fifty-yards to keep the runway dry. #47 found herself at the entrance of the hanger. She grabbed the grate and pushed up; it moved. She did not know where to go, so she decided it would be better to wait until she could hear some activity. She made use of her time and thought of a plan, while she had some food from her backpack. She was listening to her stomach and thought of #43, and smiled.

#47 closed her eyes, after having a few rice cakes and a sip of water. She needed some rest and what safer place to rest than in the shade of a hanger. She was awakened with the sound of a turbo-prop airplane, just feet away from the grate. If it had stopped on top of the grate, she would have been stuck inside the drain with no way out; somebody was watching over her and she thanked God.

The sound of high heels and the smell of a cheap cigar made its way to the ears and nose of #47. Another man walked up to greet them saying, "Welcome to the Complex, Senior Lopez. I hope your flight wasn't long." "When does the meeting begin?" asked Lopez. "Five o'clock sharp, and the bidding starts at five- fifteen," said the man. "Good, I want to be in the air by six o'clock," replied Lopez.

#47 heard them walk away; there were no other sounds, so she pushed the grate up and pulled herself out. She was stiff from being in that position and welcomed the ability to walk or run. The plane door was open with the folding steps that did not touch the floor. #47 made her way up the steps to find the pilot still sitting in his seat. He did not hear #47, as she entered the plane. #47 put her arm around his neck and he was out, within a minute. Now, she had to find anything that would be of use; she found a laptop, cash, and booze. The laptop went into her backpack, along with the cash. She took the booze and poured some of it on the pilot's shirt and put the bottle between his legs on the floor. #47 looked out of the plane and saw a door that led to the inside of another building. She would have to find somewhere to hide, but still be able to get some information for her mission. She had to move and leave no trace that she was there; she felt bad about the pilot for about a second, and then stepped out of the plane. She made her way to the door, and quickly looked inside, to see that the room was filling up with couples and men with brief cases and guns. #47 looked up and saw that there was room for her body to get above the crowd. The trick was getting there, before she was found. There was an air duct just off to the side of the room. She had to back-track to find a way inside. #47 found the mechanical room and a way to get inside the room; she just had to be quiet. It was just about five o'clock when all the doors were closed. People were still talking, when someone made an announcement that the bidding will start in a few minutes. #47 used that time to get into position, without a sound. She looked through the air grate; she had a front row seat. A small and simple stage was rolled out to the center of the floor, where a crowd started to gather around.

The bidding started, as three young, beautiful women dressed in bra and panties and heels stepped up onto the stage. They were lined up with numbers on their hips. As a number was called out, the young woman took one step forward and looked straight ahead, with no emotion on her face. A man with a camera, wearing a headset, walked near the lady and told her to smile for the camera. Number 3 smiled, as bids came in; sold for forty-five thousand. Number 5 stepped up and looked straight ahead. After a minute; sold for thirty thousand.

Number 6 stepped up and did a turnaround that showed her backside and smiled. Again, after a minute; sold for fifty-seven thousand. A man in the back, jumped up and down, happy that he had won the bid. Next, there were small children whose ages ranged from five to nine years old. #47 got mad. She was ready to kill someone, as she watched when they were sold; the prices went into the hundreds-of-thousands of dollars. It was five-forty-five when things started to slow down. The sale of drugs, by the ton, were being sold, along with favors from U.S. politicians, Law Enforcement and DOJ. It made sense to #47; they were the ones that made and enforced policy.

The last thing up for bidding was Military Intelligence from China. #47 could not wrap her head around what she had just heard; and yet, here were people paying to get country's top secrets from China. That information had been stolen by using spies within our own government; the bidding was into the millions; if not billions of dollars.

Senior Lopez and his female friend walked out of the room smiling. He had bought enough drugs from China to sell, which would make him another one- hundred-billion dollars. That was enough to buy off all the mayors and governors and any other Politician in the United States. He had a seat at the table of the One World Order.

#47 stayed in the air vent until the room cleared. She heard a man yell and then a gun shot. Senior Lopez had found his pilot fumbling to find the bottle of booze on the floor. He smelled of booze and dragged him out of the plane and shot him. He asked for another pilot to fly him home. A man ran up and offered his services. Lopez asked him if he drank. "No, Senior Lopez," came the reply, "Never have, never will." Lopez replied, "You are hired for two-hundred-thousand and keep your hands to yourself." "Yes Sir," replied the pilot.

#47 waited until she did not hear anyone before she made her way back to the mechanical room. Once there, she did a quick look around to find the place empty. A few guards were still on the property and there was a small truck parked in the hanger. #47 knew that there were more people on site, but she did not want to leave anything that could alert anyone that she did not belong there. She watched two men drag the dead body of the pilot next to a truck, and lifted him into the back. Both men got into the truck and started to leave, when #47 thought that it was a good way to leave the Complex unnoticed. She ran and jumped into the back and landed on the dead pilot. She was not heard, and that is all that mattered at this time.

Things were going fine, until she realized that she was heading further into Mexico, and the truck was slowing down to make a turn on a dirt road. She had to get off the truck fast or kill them. She jumped out of the truck and rolled away from the road. She watched as the truck continued; the dirt road left a small dust trail as it got further away.

#47 walked North; far away from the road, with her head covered, not wanting to be found. She walked several miles before she crossed paths with a boy and his mother. She was carrying a gallon of water and the boy was holding a stick and hitting weeds as he walked next to his mother. The woman stopped and offered her a drink of water. In return, #47 offered her two rice cakes and a hundred-dollar bill. The woman did not want the money and gave it back to her. Then #47 saw a phone in her bag and asked to use it or buy it. The woman smiled and handed her the phone; it had two bars, showing it still had service. #47 called the number that was given her. Someone answered the phone and asked her to hold the phone up to the sky, as high as she could, for as long as she could. A few minutes passed and #47 looked at the phone; it had one bar left as she shut it off. #47 gave the woman a stack of one-hundred-dollar bills. The woman kissed her hand and picked up her son and smiled. The woman and her son both waved and smiled as they walked away. #47 stood in the same spot and watched them until they were gone from sight.

#47 sat in a small clearing with her legs crossed and waited; it was nearly dark when she felt the wind and then the sound of a helicopter coming down from the dark sky. A spotlight hit her as she waved her arms and the light was turned off. A large man helped her inside and told her to strap in; it was going to be a very fast ride. #47 was happy to hear the English language spoken. She saw military uniforms and a large man wearing a Lady Justice pin on his collar. Mr. Jefferson had come through for her, and she was safe; her mission was complete.

16

ALWAYS A BRIDESMAID
NEVER A BRIDE

#47 FOUND HERSELF sitting in front of a few older gentlemen at a long table with Mr. Jefferson. They were introduced as Mr. Lincoln, Mr. Kennedy, and Mr. Jackson. These were not the original Presidents, of course, but as she was told before, their real names were of no consequence. They were part of the Justice Council and that did matter. Her mission was more than a success. The information that she was able to retrieve was the catalyst to start the Justice Seekers on a national level.

The criminal element and proof of crimes being committed, were beyond comprehension; the laptop was easily hacked and computer IPs were traced. The Council was able to stop or empty many of the bank transactions that were ready to go through; they were able to net over one-hundred-billion dollars. The Mexican cartels were missing their money and payments. All the off shore accounts were frozen until an International Investigation could be done. The information was damning for most of the politicians and bankers on the list. This was just the tip of the iceberg. The list of outside donors, from around the world, was proof that the One World Order was already in place. They had deep-pockets and most members of the United Nations had been bought and paid for, awaiting orders. Not one single U.S. agency was clear of any wrong doing; FBI, CIA, NSA, CDC, DHS, parts of Congress and the Senate, Secret Service, and the DOJ. Most of the corruption came from the top levels. There was buying and selling of Top-Secret information or Classified Information to the highest bidder; trading oil and minerals and nuclear plans and parts to terrorist states.

#47 was able to understand the scope of the damage that was happening to the United States and she wanted to be part of the good, and to bring justice to "We the People," before they would no longer be free. #47 felt a weight was on her shoulders. She did not understand how so few, could possibly make a difference. She had trained all her life to be the Black Dragon; to be the best at everything she did. The Justice Council would need a thousand Black Dragons just to make a dent in the criminal element of this country. Mr. Jefferson saw #47, and felt and saw the concern on her face. He talked to her and told her that he did not need an army, just a few believers to carry the flag; the rest will follow. "We need leaders like you; fearless warriors that want justice. You will clear a path for others to follow and set an example; train them as if their life would depend on it, because it will. Your mission is over, and you will soon meet others that will help you. They will be Justice Seekers, and all of you will work together and carry the burden of dispensing Justice; to carry a message to all the criminals, big or small, foreign, or domestic. "Justice Served" will be your mantra," said Mr. Jefferson. #47 believed him and said that she misses having #43 by her side, watching her back. Mr. Jefferson said that there would be many more to take her place and not to feel sad because she had made her choice and we must support her; otherwise, why are we here doing this? #47 looked at him and told him that he was like a father who watches over his children, just wanting them to be strong and free. As #47 got up to leave, the Justice Council stood up and bowed at the waist, showing her their gratitude. #47 bowed back, saying it was an honor to serve them. Mr. Jefferson walked with #47 to the door, and said that he would be at the wedding. He had to walk Grace down the aisle. He was a substitute for Grace's father, who could not make it because of his present position in the ranks of the Justice Council. "And you?" #47 smiled and said, "Always the bridesmaid, never the bride."

A few days had passed, and #47 (Kat) thought about her friend, Grace. She needed to talk to her and get dates and times down and start doing the things that bride's maids do. She had no clue what to do, so she started thinking about people that she could call upon for some help. The list was very short so she called Summer, Jim's girlfriend. Luck was with her that day. Her call to Jim was fruitful; he had a lot of information to pass on to her. Buck and Grace had decided to go to Las Vegas to get married. Grace knew her father could not walk her down the aisle, due to his involvement in the Justice Council, so to be fair, she opted out of a formal wedding and let everyone know that it would be a friends-only wedding. Kat still wanted to be a part of the wedding plans, and Grace was not going to let her best friend just stand there and hold flowers. Kat and Summer were going to meet later that day to talk with Grace so they all could make plans.

It was decided by all, that the the trip to Las Vegas was a go; a road-trip to the city that never sleeps, was in for a wedding; then back to the Trail End for a real party, with an open bar and a band. The plan was to find a small chapel and a hotel for three days and then get back on the road. Kat would be helping Grace find the right dress and a few odds and ends for the wedding couple's room. The hotel was the Hilton's Honeymoon Suite, with two extra rooms on the top floor. Kat had her own room and Jim and Summer had their own room. Mr.

Jefferson said he would be staying at the Bellagio; he had a few things he wanted to do for an old friend.

The day was set and everyone had all the things that were needed for the wedding; dresses and suits, flowers; all the paper work was done, money to the Chaplain, and a small reception room, with cake and food ordered and paid. Kat shared her room with Grace until the wedding day, which was a good thing, because Kat wanted to spend some time with her before she was gone from the Justice Seekers. Grace was following her heart and her desire to be a wife and maybe with some luck, a mother, down the road. Grace told Kat that she wanted to live in Colorado or Wyoming, in some wide-open space so she could see her surroundings. Immediately, Kat told her that she was still thinking like a warrior. Grace said that Buck wanted the same thing. Kat said that they both thought like warriors and fight like it also. Grace laughed and said Buck would never back down from a fight; he would rather take a whipping and learn from it, than walk away. I guess that is why he is good at bull riding.

Jim asked Buck if he wanted to go out and have a few drinks before his wedding day. Buck told him he wanted to stay in and not be hung over on his wedding day; he wanted everything to be prefect. Instead, he wanted to go over his wedding vows. He wanted to make her dreams come true and did not care how hard he had to work to keep his promises. Jim smiled at him and told him that he was doing Grace justice, because she was a great catch.

Two doors down, Kat asked the same thing of Grace. Grace did not want to go out either; she just wanted to make sure everything was perfect. Grace asked Kat if her scar would show. Kat looked at where she was shot, and there was only a faint scar and that was clearing up each day that passed. Kat said if she were to put a little make up on it, it would be invisible. Grace asked for Kat's hand, and put her challenge coin, with the bullet, in her hand. Kat said, "Do me the honor and save this coin. Remember that it was this coin, and you, that saved my life. I will always be a Justice Seeker and I will always be with you in spirit." Kat gave Grace a hug and told her that she was the best partner she had ever had, which was true.

Grace told her that she would stay in close contact whenever possible, once they figured out where they were going to plant some roots. Grace told her that she would always know where she is, and what she is up to, because she had someone on the inside; but you did not hear that from me. Kat smiled and said that she already knew that Mr. Jefferson had a soft spot for his people.

The wedding day was finally here; Grace was dressed in a beautiful white dress, wearing cowboy boots. Buck was dressed in a white shirt and black cowboy hat and boots. Everybody was dressed in cowboy attire, except Mr. Jefferson. He wore a blue suit, had a camera in his hands, and walked around took photos of the guests and bride. He could have been a professional photographer the way he looked through the lens and followed the light to his best advantage. At the end of the day, the only person that had been missing in the photos was Kat; it was done by design. The photos of the bride and groom cutting the cake and the first dance, was all done to keep everyone safe.

When everything was done and the bride and groom were ready to exit, everyone gave their hugs and blessings. Grace stood in the middle of their wedding suite and looked at all the presents around their small table with strawberries and champagne. Buck was surprised at the number of presents around the table, and stopped when he saw a small briefcase with a ribbon on it. Grace looked around and told him to step away from the briefcase until she could look at it. Buck stepped aside and asked if she thought it was a bomb? She said, "No, I am just careful," as she looked closely at the markings on the briefcase. She knew it was okay; there was a small tag saying, "The Council". Grace opened the briefcase and Buck saw that there was a Deed and some papers that needed signing. There was another small envelope addressed to Buck and Grace saying, "Follow your Hearts." The Deed was of Buck's old home, that his father sold. Someone had bought the ranch from a foreign corporation with all the mineral and water rights. It was now Buck's ranch to do whatever he wanted. He did not understand; his father walked away from the ranch with a load of cash in his hand and he had given Buck part of the money. That is how he had bought Grace's wedding ring. There was a note saying that the corporation had made a very bad mistake and wanted to make amends to any of the former residents. A check was enclosed for any inconvenience they had caused, with a full refund. The amount was over by two-hundred-thousand dollars. Once Buck signed the papers, they would own the ranch free and clear. This was a huge start in the right direction. Grace only knew of one person that could have done this, and in her heart, she thanked Mr. Jefferson and The Justice Council. Grace also knew that Kat had something to do with it, but she did not want to know how and hugged Buck.

Jim, Summer, and Kat walked the strip, and checked out all the gambling and noises coming from casinos. Kat looked at all the different foods that were available. Summer looked at all the stores with dresses and beauty aids, while Jim wanted to try his hand at some gambling. By the end of the night, everybody had done what they wanted; Kat ate at an Asian fusion restaurant, Summer bought a new purse and Jim walked out of a Texas Hold-em card game five-hundred-dollars ahead. It was a good night all around. Grace and Buck had left word that they would see them at the Trails End Bar in three days and to be ready to dance. Mr. Jefferson was on his way to Colorado to put #38 into play; it was time start the Justice Seekers. There was enough information on the books to keep them busy and the nation would soon hear about the Justice Seekers; at least the criminals would be on notice.

At the Trails End Bar, everybody was on time, and the band played until dawn the next day. The manager said it had been the best day in its history and the first time for a wedding reception. Mr. Jefferson left a thank you envelope with the manager to help him out with the cost of the open bar.

Back in Colorado, two cowboys were sitting by a fire joined by their wives. Daryel was sitting with a pillow under his leg. Jace was passing another beer to Daryel and asked, "Ever wonder about those two investigators?" Daryel looked around and said, "Don't know anything about any investigators," but I will say that we have not had any more problems around here. "Yup," said Jace, better left alone. I bet we could turn on the news and make a pretty good guess about things. Ronda asked, "Daryel, are you ready to move it inside"? Daryel replied, "Why not, and let's turn on the news." Jace laughed a little and looked over his shoulder as they went inside. "You just never know where that little lady in black will turn up. I'm sure glad she is on our side." "Things are bound to get better, but it is going to get worse, before it gets better. It is going to take someone to bring us hope and justice and I pray that it has already started," said Jace. "Amen to that," came a reply from the kitchen, as Lesli and Ronda opened a beer for themselves.

In another part of Colorado, Ben and Jill were excited that they were going to dinner at the Hilton Hotel. They knew something was brewing. They both had just finished their training and they were ready for anything; plus, they had their Lady Justice pins.

THE END